for

Witches

and

Spellcasters

About the Author

Mya Om (Michigan) has traveled around the world. A lifelong witch, she was initiated into the Craft in 1998, after studying both Dianic and American Eclectic Wiccan traditions.

To Write to the Author

If you wish to contact the author or would like more information about this book, please write to the author in care of Llewellyn Worldwide and we will forward your request. Both the author and publisher appreciate hearing from you and learning of your enjoyment of this book and how it has helped you. Llewellyn Worldwide cannot guarantee that every letter written to the author can be answered, but all will be forwarded. Please write to:

Mya Om
c/o Llewellyn Worldwide
2143 Wooddale Drive
Woodbury, MN 55125-2989

Please enclose a self-addressed stamped envelope for reply,
or $1.00 to cover costs. If outside the U.S.A., enclose an
international postal reply coupon.

Many of Llewellyn's authors have websites with additional information and resources. For more information, please visit our website at:

www.llewellyn.com

Energy Essentials

for

Witches

and

Spellcasters

Mya Om

Llewellyn Publications
Woodbury, Minnesota

First Edition
Second Printing, 2010

Cover background fire image © PhotoDisc
Cover design by Ellen Dahl
Editing by Lee Lewis Walsh

Llewellyn is a registered trademark of Llewellyn Worldwide Ltd.

Library of Congress Cataloging-in-Publication Data
Om, Mya.
  Energy essentials for witches and spellcasters / Mya Om.—1st ed.
      p. cm.
  Includes bibliographical references.
  ISBN 978-0-7387-1550-6
  1. Witchcraft. 2. Charms. I. Title.
  BF1566.O53 2009
  133.4'3—dc22
                                                                    2009017474

Llewellyn Publications
A Division of Llewellyn Worldwide Ltd.
2143 Wooddale Drive
Woodbury, MN 55125-2989
www.llewellyn.com

Printed in the United States of America

Contents

Acknowledgments

I would like to dedicate this book to my grandmothers—I wish they were here today to see it.

I would like to thank all the people who have helped get me to this point! You know who you are, but in case you don't, Lj, Angie, Ash, Shell, Vickie, and the online people on SOTW and Briar Rose. I very much appreciate and love all of you.

Introduction

I FIRST ENCOUNTERED WICCA AND American witchcraft when I was young, and I was drawn to them from the very first instant. They filled a hole in my life that was created by my family's move from Jordan to America, and they allowed me to refine the skills I'd been taught as a child at the knee of my great-grandmother.

My Jeda was a Gypsy, although not in the way that Americans think of Gypsies or in the way associated with the Roma or Romany peoples. She was an authentic Gypsy; her family, my family, traces its lineage back to the first people who left Egypt and traveled, unfettered by the demands of a homeland, throughout Asia Minor and Europe. The stories that she told me of her childhood, traveling throughout the Ottoman Empire and Eastern Europe, are the cornerstone of my magick. The teachings she passed on to me about life in general, and spells in particular, have allowed me to create a unique and powerful synthesis of Wicca and folk magic that consistently provides amazing results.

The women in my family never called themselves witches. The term "witch" isn't understood very well in the Middle East—at least not as the word is used today. Jeda was a healer, an astrologer, a matchmaker, and a wonderful cook. By the time I was born—her oldest great-granddaughter—she was old, well into her nineties. Thankfully, she had a quick mind, and her nimble hands could roll a cigarette in under thirty seconds flat. She loved to talk and I was an eager listener. In summer, I would wake up before dawn just so I could help her make the bread for the day. This was our special time together, when I learned about the world from her stories. She imparted so much wisdom and knowledge to me, although I didn't understand it at the time.

To her, everything was a ritual, from the deliberate way she made coffee to the tinctures she sold to young women hoping to find love. Even her stories were a ritual. First, she would roll a cigarette between her thumb and forefinger, then pour cups of perfectly steeped, hot and sweet tea, one for her and one for me. It seemed that she always knew the moment the tea was perfect and we wouldn't begin until then. Over a breakfast of hot tea, warm bread dipped in olive oil, and perhaps some grapes, she would talk. She told me, her eager audience, stories of her childhood, the Turks, the many wars she'd lived through and, most of all, about her people. Tales of her mother, of Palestine, of her travels as a child, and of finally settling in a valley a mere ten miles away from the Jordanian border with Israel. I grew up there, in the shadow of Israel, in the place considered so holy by the great religions of Christianity, Islam, and Judaism. It was there that I learned the basics of being a witch.

My family had been in America for less than a year and I was barely in high school when I first encountered Wicca. In my new life here, I was missing so much that I wanted to reclaim. There are no little rituals in America. Tea comes in individual-sized bags and is made in single cups, and the water is heated in the microwave. Coffee percolates by dripping from a machine, and no cardamom pods scent the air. Instead, nondairy creamer is mixed in by the spoonful and a mug is downed on the run. There are no family breakfasts here; hummus comes from a can, not a Lebanese storefront up the street, and there are no fried eggs or goat cheese. Fresh bread, baked at dawn and eaten with oil pressed from our own olives, was a luxury of the past.

A friend of mine called herself a witch and I didn't understand what that meant. I don't think she understood what it meant, either, but she lent me a book, *The Spiral Dance* by Starhawk. She had stolen the book from her mother's library. Of course, she had chosen the biggest and most complex book in an effort to impress me. Reading this book changed my life. In the introduction, I read about a young Jewish girl who grew up with a family that sounded just like mine. She tried, just as I was trying, to understand the differences between what she felt was real and what she was told was real.

I didn't understand everything in the book—some of the concepts were beyond my limited knowledge and some exercises were way over my head—but I liked what I did understand. Interestingly enough, much of what the author described I recognized as the common practices of my childhood, the rites of my great-grandmother. The book allowed me to make a needed leap in awareness, coming to the realization that if what Starhawk described was witchcraft, then I was a witch and Jeda was, too. Here I could reinvent what I'd lost in my new world.

I was sad to give the book back to my friend, but I couldn't keep it and her mother had noticed its absence. It was around my birthday and I had a little money. In high school, every dollar is cherished like it might be your last, especially when you aren't old enough to drive or have a job. I decided that I would spend my money, not on a movie or new clothes, but to buy my own book.

Unfortunately, at the time, *The Spiral Dance* was out of print. What I ended up with, chosen by my friend from the shelves of the New Age section at the bookstore, was a spell book. I won't share with you its title or author, but I am sure that you have seen many like it. It included some three hundred spells, all arranged in alphabetical order, covering everything from addiction to wishes. The book told the reader that, if you could see your goal in your mind's eye and you followed the instructions of the spell, whatever you desired would become yours. I was excited; finally, I would have all the stuff I wanted! The boy in algebra class who didn't know I was alive would ask me out. My parents would stop harassing me to clean my room. I would have money, a car, straight As, and life would be great. The book was an investment, I thought, one that would pay off in the end—but I was wrong.

At the time, I didn't understand why the spells didn't work; after all, I followed the instructions. I closed my eyes and concentrated on my desire—I mean, I *visualized* my goals. I lit the candles, I said the words. I discarded the remnants of my spell in an appropriate location at the correct time. I even spent most of the hour in algebra class reinforcing my desire for that boy to notice me—so much so that I ended up with a C, and still no interest from him. So much for that spell! What was I missing? It took me years to realize what was wrong: why the spells didn't work and why, when they did work, they didn't work quite right, or they had the opposite result of what I intended. The difference between what I did then and what I do now is *energy*. It's a simple enough difference, but it packs a huge punch.

This book is written from a Wiccan point of view, with lots of folk and Gypsy elements added in. I am a Wiccan by choice, inclination, and force of will. However, you don't have to be Wiccan to practice witchcraft and not all Wiccans actually cast spells. As you become more experienced, you'll realize that there is a difference between Wicca as a religion and witchcraft as a skill. Personally, I believe in the God and Goddess working in balance, and I believe in the Wiccan Rede. I believe in reincarnation, circle casting, corner calling, guardians, and divine assistance. I also believe that, while all these elements can help you with spellwork if you believe in them, *they are not necessary for successful spells.*

I am not writing this book to teach you about Wicca; many other authors have done this much better than I ever could. Even so, one of the foundation statements in Wicca applies to our purpose here: "To know, to will, to dare and to keep silent." The "knowing" is easy: you read books, you talk to people, and you begin to assimilate the cosmology of Wicca and the skills of witchcraft. "Keeping silent" is easy, too; most people, particularly new witches, don't tend to run around talking about their lifestyle or their spells. The other two elements, "to will" and "to dare," are critical to casting spells that actually work (more about that later on).

For the most part, this book is targeted toward solitary witches, although most of the exercises can be retooled for group or coven work. That being said, I believe spells are by necessity solitary and selfish. After all, it is *your* will being done. Spells performed as a group are harder for several reasons. First, attaining group mind is hard, and second, reinforcing group will is very hard. Finally, a group is only as strong as its weakest link. It takes monumental trust between members to cast spells as a group. I have a group of people I've known for years, and even though I will happily celebrate full moons and holidays with them, I will only do spellwork with a select few. That doesn't mean that you shouldn't do spells in a group; just be aware that there are more obstacles to overcome.

This book begins with the foundations of spellwork. It covers the basic concepts and includes exercises designed to help you determine the best approach to your spell. It will teach you how to connect with energy, and how to reinforce it and manipulate it for the most effective outcome. We'll break down some traditional spells and rewrite them for best results, and you'll learn how to create your own spells. It concludes with some tips that have helped me.

If you're like me, you're probably skeptical, and rightly so. I mean, look around: how many books in the New Age section promise results? How many of them supposedly teach you how to do a spell? They tell you that you'll have everything you ever wanted and then let you down once you've bought them. This book won't teach you how to make Joe in algebra class fall in love with you. Instead, it will teach you how to draw love into your life; you might not get Joe, but the person you end up with will probably be better for you. My purpose here is to teach you how to cast spells that work well, and work as intended, to make your desires reality. Then it's all up to you—your actions and your beliefs will determine the outcome. Good luck!

one

Foundations
of Spellwork

THE PREMISE BEHIND THIS BOOK is simple: anyone can cast a powerful and successful spell.

I know that this sounds like an unrealistic claim, but the truth of the matter is that each and every person has the ability, if not the knowledge, to cast a spell. The very essence of spellwork is the belief of the witch in the power of the spell, and in the spell's ability to manifest results. This sounds easy, but trust me—it's the hardest part of magick.

A spell can be defined as a stated desire reinforced with will and fed by energy. Take away the energy or weaken the will and all that's left is a few lines of poorly rhymed words. A witch, male or female, needs to maintain a connection with each spell that reinforces the intent of the working and the desired result. The minute the witch falters in his or her belief in the ability of the spell to succeed, he or she risks the failure of the spell and even a possible negative outcome. Spellwork is all about energy; what the caster puts in, the caster gets back. For the more scientific among you, try to think of it in terms of the law of conservation of energy. If you put in doubt, you get back failure, or, at worst, the opposite of what your spell intended. This means that, as a witch, you must be very careful in both thought and actions. Everything you do, say, or think must be "on message" for your desired goal. Anything else means failure. Does that sound harsh? It is; I can't sugarcoat it for you.

Here's an example. For years I wanted to lose weight and I cast several spells to do so. At the time the spell was cast, I was confident that it would work. But the next day, when I looked in the mirror, doubts began to sneak in. I would think, "Ugh! I'm so fat, I'll never be thin." At the time, I didn't understand the power of thought. I would wait, doing little things to lose weight, but each morning when I faced myself in the mirror, I would think, "Ugh! I'm so fat, I'll never be thin." When I didn't see results after several months, I would wonder why the spell didn't work. I knew magick worked; I had other spells work for me during that time. *So what am I doing wrong?* I wondered. After a while I tried again, with similar results. Finally, I became frustrated and stopped casting spells to lose weight.

Several years later I had a breakthrough. I had an acquaintance who was one of the most powerful witches I knew. She never called herself a witch; in fact, she characterized herself as a charismatic Christian. (Surprised? Don't be.) She told me that a person had to "speak their own reality into existence." She believed that God wants each of us to be successful and wants to give people what they need and desire. According to her, God would only respond to his Word, repeated to him in supplication. So she had a collection of Bible verses that she repeated in prayer each morning and evening. That I could understand; after all, what is a prayer, if not a type of spell? But here is the interesting part—she adamantly refused to speak or think anything contrary to her stated goals. She refused even to sing along to lyrics of a song on the radio if the words were contrary to her goal. This made me think, *What if there is something to this?*

I decided to look back at spells I'd cast that had worked and examine my attitude during the time it took the spell to manifest. (This can be very helpful and I suggest you do the same.) I found that, almost exclusively, the spells that brought about the best results were the ones I'd reinforced with a constant belief in their success. The spells I'd cast with only limited results were the ones I'd forgotten about or hadn't put any effort into after casting. And the spells that were the most spectacular failures were the ones I had thought about negatively, like the weight loss example above.

To test this theory, I decided to recast a spell to obtain extra money that I had done several months prior. It was intended to bring me the funds for a home improvement project I desperately wanted to work on. But every time I thought about the project or got a bill, I remembered thinking that the money to complete the project would never come. Predictably, the money did not manifest during the time period I had set. So I recast the spell, and had a chance to test my theory the next day when three large bills came in the mail. In the past, I would've looked at these expenses and thought, *There goes my extra money; I'm not going to have enough to . . .* Instead, I looked at the bills and said aloud, "Money will come to pay this. All my needs are met."

This new mindset was hard! I would catch myself starting to fall back into my old patterns. But each time I did, I would say the affirmation out loud, sometimes several times. I fixed this goal in my mind and decided that nothing was going to stop me from reaching it. Less than thirty days later, I received money from a very unexpected source, a bonus. The windfall covered all the expenses of the home improvement project and a little extra.

Perhaps it was a fluke, I thought. So I tried it again, on several different things, with similar results. Then came the time when I decided finally to try this new method with weight loss—my magical nemesis. I hid the scale to remove the temptation to weigh myself constantly. I put the exercise equipment in plain view and wrote a new affirmation on several pieces of paper. One I stuck to the bathroom mirror, one I placed in my bedroom, and the last I taped to the exercise machine. This was the hardest thing; weight loss had eluded me for years. Even in high school I was heavier than I wanted to be, and by the time I cast the spell, I was at almost three hundred pounds. When you get to that point, even doctors give up on you losing weight without surgery. But within two months, I had lost twenty pounds, and over the next year I lost almost a hundred pounds. I won't tell you what I weigh today, but suffice to say I credit the spell with spectacular results.

I'm sure you're thinking that this happened because I changed my lifestyle, and you'd be right. I exercised, I tried to eat right, and I repeated my affirmation seven or eight times a day. The spell wasn't meant to make me wake up suddenly fifty pounds lighter. It was meant to give me the ability to stick with my plan, to reinforce my will, and to help me reach my goals.

That is what this book can do for you. It will provide a framework from which you can build, energize, and reinforce spells to get spectacular results.

Next, we'll work through a set of three exercises designed to clarify your intent. Be sure to do them in order. At the end, you should have a better understanding of yourself, your desires and their consequences, and the baggage you might be carrying that can affect the success of your spells.

What do I want?

For this you will need:

> *Twenty minutes of alone time*
> *A pen or pencil*
> *Paper or a small notebook*

Find a place and time where you won't be easily disturbed. Pick somewhere where you'll be comfortable and where you'll be able to write things down. Take a few minutes to get centered and to release the tensions and worries of everyday life. Take some calm, relaxing breaths, and leave everything at the door. Be at peace here.

Next, think about something that you need or want to have right now. This can be something that you've done spells for, or something that you might want to do a spell for; it can also be something that you'd never consider working magick for. When you have the desire clear in your mind, write it down at the top of the first page.

Now, under that, write out the following questions, leaving room to write the answers.

- *If I got what I wanted today, what impact would this have on my life?*
- *Who else would be affected by my actions?*
- *Does this fit in with my long-term goals?*

- *Will it make me happy? Why or why not?*
- *If I didn't get this desire, what would happen?*
- *Am I willing to put in the work needed to get it?*

Take as long as you need to respond to all the questions thoroughly. If you're like me, you should be able to fill several pages with the possible ramifications.

Finally, there's one more question:

Is it worth it to go after this want or need?

You probably know the answer to this one already, but be sure to re-read what you've written before making a decision. If the answer is yes, and you're willing to put your all into it, then magick can help you. If the answer is no, or you're not willing to put the work into it, then magick can't help. Magick is not a shortcut! You can't just recite rhyming words and expect that your world will change (that only works on TV). In order to get real results, you have to be willing to put in the necessary effort, energy, will, and follow-through. If you're not willing or able to do that, your spells won't work.

Why don't I already have what I want or need?

Once you've identified a need and examined whether it's something that you're willing to work toward, next you need to recognize why this need is not being met right now.

For this exercise, you're going have to ask yourself some difficult questions and be willing to answer them honestly. Magick doesn't work well if you aren't honest with yourself about your motives and about what you really, *really* want. You need to understand where you're coming from before you can determine how to get to where you want to go.

For this exercise you will need:

Five to ten minutes of alone time
A pen or pencil
Paper or a small notebook

Again, choose a place where you won't be disturbed and take a few moments to get centered. Now, thinking about the need or want you identified in the previous exercise, answer the following questions:

- *Is this a new need/want or is it ongoing?*

- *Am I doing anything that is perpetuating the situation?*

- *Is what I want/need a symptom of a bigger issue that will hinder the success of this working in some way?*

- *Does something else need to change before I can have this want/need fulfilled?*

Sometimes it is easy to overlook the underlying issues surrounding the reasons for our desires and needs. In this consumer-minded world, we are often confronted with perceptions of how our lives should be—the kind of car we should own, what our kids should study, or the type of job we should have. When confronting the idealized fantasy, we overlook the good parts of our lives. This can lead to too much focus on what we should have, rather than what we do have. This focus can overwhelm the positive aspects of things in our lives and act as a block that stops us from actually reaching our goals.

Before taking any steps, it is very important to seriously consider all the ramifications associated with the possible outcome of your spell, beyond what can be seen on the surface. Ask yourself, what are the long-term impacts? Is there a different direction you can take? And really probe and ask the hard questions—treat yourself like a subject in an interrogation. If you would ask a particular question of a stranger who came to you with the same question, ask it of yourself, and be honest with the answer.

Most of all, remember to focus not only on what you want now, but also on your goals for the future.

EXERCISE 1.3

How can magick help me get what I want or need?

Here we'll look at the possible ways in which magick can work to bring about your desire.

For this exercise you will need:

Five to ten minutes of alone time

A pen or pencil

Paper or a small notebook

Choose a place where you won't be disturbed and take a few moments to get centered. Start by drawing a vertical line down the middle of the page so you have two columns. Label one "Positive ways I could reach my goal" and the other "Negative ways I could reach my goal." Take a few minutes to really think about the different possibilities. Keep in mind that we're not thinking about various types of spells here; keep the focus on real-world actions you could take. Magick will always take the path of least resistance to bring you what you want.

Now let's work through all three exercises together, using a desire nearly everyone can relate to.

Exercise 1.1: What do I want?

My desire is to lose weight.

If I got what I wanted today, what impact would this have on my life?

I would weigh less, so my health would probably improve. I would feel better about myself since I would look better. I could wear those jeans I've been holding onto since high school. Losing weight would improve my self-image.

Who else would be affected by my actions?

My first instinct is to say only myself, but my friends might be affected because they're jealous (wouldn't that make me feel good!). My family would be affected if I go on a diet and don't buy sweets or cook the food they like. My coworkers, if I don't go out to lunch with them anymore and start bringing a bag lunch to watch my calories. The burger place where I used to buy my lunch, since their revenue would decrease. The gym I join to exercise more, since their revenue would increase.

Does this fit in with my long-term goals?

Yes, because one of my goals is to be healthier.

Will it make me happy? Why or why not?

Losing the weight would make me happy, but the dieting and exercise needed to do so won't make me happy.

I'll be happy because I'll be able to wear my old jeans; my self-image will improve, and so will my health. So overall I would be happy.

If I didn't get this desire, what would happen?

I would still be heavier than I would like. This would affect my health over time, and I might gain more weight. The jeans I'm waiting to wear again might get eaten by moths in the back of my closet. My family members might gain weight, since I will continue to buy sweets and cook unhealthy foods.

Am I willing to put in the work needed to get it?

Yes, because I need to lose weight to be healthy and my health is very important to me. But since I don't have a lot of time to exercise, I'm going to have to change my diet and I know I'm going to need help to keep me working toward this goal.

Bottom line: This goal is important to me, and I'm willing to do the necessary work to make it happen. No revision to the goal is needed.

Exercise 1.2: Why don't I already have what I want or need?

Is this a new need/want or is it ongoing?

Ongoing and long-term.

Am I doing anything that is perpetuating the situation?

Yes, my current diet is not as healthy as it could be and my time management skills need to be improved to make room for exercise.

Is what I want/need a symptom of a bigger issue that will hinder the success of this working in some way?

Yes, the bigger issue is my general lifestyle and my time management.

Does something else need to change before I can have this want/need fulfilled?

My lifestyle needs to change and if it doesn't, I won't lose any weight. Any spell to lose weight won't help me until I change my eating habits and make time to exercise.

Bottom line: Your goal needs to be clear, specific, and accurate. Therefore, the goal needs to be restated as "I want to change my lifestyle by eating healthier and finding time to exercise." (If your clarified goal is far different than your original goal, you might want to go back and do exercise 1.1 again.)

Exercise 1.3: How can magick help me get what I want or need?

Positive ways I could reach my goal:

> *I could exercise to lose weight*
> *I could cut calories and watch what I eat*
> *I could cut out junk food*
> *I could eat more fruits and veggies*

Negative ways I could reach my goal:

> *I could get sick*
> *I could starve myself by not eating enough*
> *I could exercise too much*

It should be clear by now that your spells are not going to work when your goals, your lifestyle, or your attitude contradict your workings. I can do a million spells to lose weight, but if I get up in the morning, look in the mirror, and say "I'm so fat, I'm never going to lose this weight!" then magick is not going to help. Similarly, if I binge on cookies, brownies, and cake, I won't reach my goals, either. The key is tying together the mundane and the magical. Think of it as approaching the battle on two fronts.

Remember that spells are delicate things. They are completely dependent on the actions and continued reinforcement of the witch to work and to grow. If you contradict the desired outcome of your spell, either through your actions or your words, you create additional barriers that your spell has to work through or around to bring you what you want. This means that your results might take longer to manifest—if they can manifest at all.

Statements like "I'm never going to lose this weight" are contrary to the stated intent of the spell. If you continue to speak and think like that, the energy you invest in the spell won't be enough to overcome the contradictory energy produced by your negative statements and they will cancel each other out. This means that the spell will fizzle and you won't see any results. Further, you run the risk that the energy put out by the negative statements will *overwhelm* the energy of the spell, to the extent that your words and thoughts not only cancel out any positive result but actually start producing negative results. So the negativity becomes its own "spell," and each bit of energy you put into thinking that you're fat adds to its power and you end up gaining ten pounds. In that case, your outcome is completely contrary to the stated intent of the original spell, but it is completely in agreement with your own statements.

Jeda was always fond of saying, "Be careful what you ask for, as you never know who will be listening." This means that if you want your spells to work, you have to stay "on message." You have to reinforce your desired outcome, not your fears or your perception of what the truth is. The idea is to get what you want, and to do that, you have to take control of your thoughts and your actions. If you can't do that, Joe in algebra class will never know you're alive. However, if you walk up to him and say hello, maybe start a conversation instead of staring longingly from across the room (which is totally creepy by the way), you might discover that he likes you too. Combine this real-world action with a powerful spell, and you might be surprised at what happens.

I found out at my five-year high school reunion that the boy in algebra had liked me too, but he'd been too shy to say anything. Of course, by that time we'd both moved on, but I can't help but wonder what would have happened if I'd acted on the spell I'd cast instead of waiting for it to act.

EXERCISE 1.4

Positive reinforcement

What you'll need for this exercise:

Five minutes a day for seven days
A pen or pencil
Two sheets of paper
A fireproof dish
A lighter
A mirror

As always, choose a place where you won't be disturbed and take a few moments to get centered. On the first sheet of paper, write out ten statements about what is wrong with your life; for example, "I never have any money." On the second sheet, write out ten statements that are the exact opposite of what you wrote on the first page; for example, "I always have the money I need."

Take a minute and re-read both lists. Which statements would you prefer to manifest in your life? How many times have you found yourself speaking aloud those negative statements on the first list? How many times have you thought them? How many times have you sighed when things didn't go your way and thought, *It's never going to change?*

What you need to do here is make a commitment: are you ready to give up the life on the first list and work toward the life on the second list? If you are, then you need to take control today and begin shaping the world to your will.

Take list A and get rid of all those negative things in your life. Burn that paper! Hold it carefully by one corner over a fireproof dish (on a fireproof surface, of course), light the opposite corner, and watch the paper burn for a moment. Drop it into the fireproof dish and say aloud, with as much emotion as you can muster, "I banish this negativity from my life."

Then pick up list B. Place the mirror in front of you (or hold it), look yourself in the eye, and read that list. Now you're sending out positivity instead of negativity.

Next, I want you to read list B to yourself, every morning for seven days, while facing yourself in the mirror. During your day, every time you find yourself making one of the statements on list A, or thinking one of them, stop and speak aloud the opposite statement. In this way you'll retake control. It may sound simplistic, but our words and thoughts really do shape our reality.

When you cast a spell, you need to make sure your words and thoughts coincide with the results you're hoping for. You don't necessarily have to constantly think about the spell and how it's working, but you can't make statements that contradict its intent. Also avoid statements like, "It didn't work, I know it didn't!" Or "Why do my spells never work?" Instead, create a positive statement that reinforces your spell's intent. This keeps the energy flowing into your spell rather than working against it.

These actions take a lot of courage, especially if you, like me, are a little shy and are afraid to step out of your comfort zone. You have to remember that courage doesn't mean that you aren't afraid; it just means that, despite the fear, you are going to take action anyway. The opposite of fear isn't courage, it's hope. With every spell you cast, you are putting hope before fear. Of course, hope without action, as Jeda always said, is laziness. "The universe doesn't reward laziness, Mya," she always said, "it laughs at it."

add emotional energy when speaking to invoke and

The worst thing in the world for my great-grandmother was to be lazy. At least once a week, Jeda would be visited by a young woman, or more accurately a young woman and her mother, with hopes that Jeda could help the girl find a husband. Marriage is very important in the Middle East. Boys and girls don't date like they do here, nor are marriages arranged. Well, not in most cases anyway. Instead, what ideally happens is boy sees girl. Boy thinks girl is pretty. Boy asks his mother who girl is. Mom finds out. If the girl is acceptable, she tells her son who the girl is. If the girl is not acceptable, she tells him that he doesn't need to know this girl. After that, mom will visit the girl's family and talk with the girl's mother. The girl's mother will talk to the girl's father. If everything is acceptable, the girl's mother will visit the boy's mother with her daughter. Then the boy and his father will visit the girl's father, and the girl and boy will finally meet after being nominally engaged. So, getting married requires a lot of networking, a good reputation, and a great deal of luck. When the girl and her mother visited, Jeda would always ask, "What have you done to find a husband?"

In most cases, the girl and her mother would have done nothing. They would have been waiting for a Cinderella-type moment, where a prince sees the girl from across the room and is smitten. Now that might work in fairy tales, but we know that in real life, unless you like look like Halle

Berry, no guy is going to fall in love with you from across the room. Now, depending on the situation, Jeda had several different solutions. The one she used most often was to read the girl's palm and then recommend wearing red (to attract attention) and going out more often, particularly to weddings, where the guests are already thinking about marriage. This always involved the girl getting out of her comfort zone and doing something to get what she wanted. To Jeda, people didn't deserve to get what they wanted if they didn't work for it.

That being said, there were instances where the girl and her mother had done everything right and still had no results. In those cases, Jeda always looked at the energy surrounding the girl and her family to see what was hindering her. Jeda never called it energy per se. To her it was more of a feeling, and 90 percent of the time she was completely correct about what was going on. In some cases, negative energy builds around a person, a family, or a situation, and it can repel change.

In the next chapter, we are going to discuss how to sense energy and how to tell if the energy surrounding you is positive or negative, so I think that it is important to describe here how negativity can surround a particular person or situation. We just talked about how sending out negative thoughts and energy can work to negate spellwork or produce results that are contrary to the stated goals of the spell. Negativity works the same way; it can build around a person or a situation until it feels like there is a cloud hanging over the person. The negativity comes from those thoughts and actions that hinder your desires.

This doesn't mean that a person surrounded by negativity is a bad person or that he or she has done bad things. It only means that the person is surrounded by bad energy. Yes, this energy can come from bad actions, but most likely it comes from self-defeating thoughts, low self-esteem, or by taking in the negativity others send toward the person. The same is true of buildings. Many people sometimes get a bad vibe when they walk into or by a particular building or have problems when moving in to a new house or apartment. This doesn't mean that the place is bad, only that it has the residue of the negativity of the people who live or used to live there.

It is very hard to break a negative cycle. Many people get stuck in the negativity, and they find themselves unable to get out. Negativity is self-perpetuating. Like a fire, it consumes everything around it, growing exponentially as more energy is created through each negative occurrence. Like a fire storm, it keeps going until there is nothing left except scorched earth and ashes. It takes a gigantic effort of will to redirect all the negativity to something positive, particularly when it is at the stage where it feels like it has consumed everything good in our lives. Many call this hitting rock bottom. The good thing about being at the bottom, or in the center of a scorched earth after the fire, is that there is nothing left for the fire to consume, so the only way to go is up.

At times like these, it feels like we should just give up, that nothing will change, and that things will always be that bad. It is this thought process that perpetuates the negativity. Part of being a witch is recognizing patterns like this and learning how to break them. Spells can help with this, as can ritual cleansings of the home, workplace, etc., but they are only part of what is needed to break the cycle. We discussed earlier that spells require a commitment to stay on message to work; our lives are the same way. For positive things to happen to us, we need to create a positive environment, not just physically, but mentally.

The gods don't want us to be miserable; they want us to be happy and successful. They've given us the tools to do that, through magick and through our will. Unfortunately they can't just *give* us success and happiness—how would we learn if they did that? If we want things to change, we have to claim those changes for ourselves. By practicing magick, we have taken the first step toward transforming our lives, but we need to follow through on the intent of our magick.

two

Sensing Energy

ENERGY IS THE BASIC BUILDING block of matter. If we examine matter on an atomic scale, we find that everything is made up of electrons, protons, and neutrons. An electromagnetic field allows the positively charged protons to attract and hold the negatively charged electrons. Since everything in the universe is made up of atoms, everything produces energy, which can be described as the output created by the attraction between oppositely charged particles. This is similar to the way a battery works. A single cell battery has a positive and a negative end. When placed into a device, say a power screwdriver, the battery completes a circuit and allows the energy stored inside the battery to flow into the tool. So if you think of a spell as a tool and energy as a battery, you can understand why most spells don't work—they're missing the battery. Unfortunately spells don't come with a troubleshooting guide, so most spellcasters never realize that the battery was not included.

Earlier, I referred to a principal tenet of Wicca: "To know, to will, to dare, and to keep silent." As I said, "to know" and "to keep silent" are relatively easy; the other two require more effort. "To will" means to use the power of your mind to affect your reality. "To dare" means that you have the follow-through to take the action needed to reach your goals. These two are often the missing pieces in spellwork. Together they direct the energy that we will be discussing throughout the rest of the book. They form the "battery" of your spell.

Magick and witchcraft are tools designed to assert the will of the individual to gain control over a tangible situation; for example, I need a hundred dollars to pay bills, so I do a spell to bring me money. The goal is to learn how to harness the energy that is all around us and use it to direct our spells to manifest real results.

Here's how it was explained to me as a child. The soul or *rooh* is made of the breath of Allah (God) trapped in animated clay (our bodies); this soul is pure energy. Each person is gifted with a portion of the same substance that makes up Allah; however, this is only a portion of Allah and it is further restricted by being trapped in a physical body. Still, it gifts those who are able to connect directly with this substance a certain degree of creative (or destructive) power. This is the same force that Allah used to create the universe and, potentially, each human has access to this power. What this means is that each person has the ability to create his or her own universe.

Essentially, we have the ability to create a positive or negative reality for ourselves, depending on how we use our energy. If you recall, in the Bible, God spoke the world into existence. It follows that if we have even a portion of God's power, our words also have power. Spells are just words that are infused with energy and reinforced by the will. And as we explored in chapter 1, negative words, if they are repeated often enough and if they are invested with enough emotion, can cause real effects in our lives. Thus we must understand that this energy exists and can be used positively or negatively, to create or to destroy.

Every part of your life, and every issue you may want to address by means of a spell, is surrounded by its own energy. To many people, using this energy for anything besides creation is evil. These people assume that we don't have the judgment as humans to fully understand the consequences of our actions and the ripple effects that we send out. You are an adult, and you are responsible for your own actions, good or bad. I have no desire to control you, and I won't waste the energy trying. So all I will say is do what you will, as long as you are willing to accept the responsibility for your actions.

As individuals we often have goals that we want to reach in our lives, and as witches we use magick as a way to help us reach these goals. Oftentimes, though, when we begin working a spell, we don't look at exactly what we want the outcome to be. Other times, we only have a limited vision of what the outcome should be, and we often fail to connect what we want right now with what our long-term goals are. So when things don't work out exactly as we planned, we blame the spell for not anticipating our needs or not foreseeing the consequences of our actions.

The absolute first step before you begin any working should be to understand the energy around your issue or goal, and to do that, you must be able to sense energy. Although most of us can't see it, nearly everyone can learn to feel it. To some it's a sensation of heat or cold, a mild shock like static electricity, or a tingle or shiver that runs down the spine. Of the very few people that can actually see energy, some perceive it as color; to me, it looks like steam rising off a hot road in summer. Although energy itself is tangible, it's notably hard to describe. I even went back to my old teacher and asked her how to write about it, and she said to me, "How do you explain color to a blind person, or music to the deaf? Some things just have to be experienced, because each person will feel it differently."

This chapter is designed to help you learn to experience energy. Sensing energy is a learned skill, not an innate "gift" that some people have and some don't. The goal here is to open up your senses and get in touch with the primal, latent energy that is all around us, all the time. Remember that working with energy is an integral part of creating spells that manifest results; prior to charging objects or activating spells, you must learn how to access energy and channel it. And before you can do that, you have to learn how to access your *own* energy—how to raise it, lower it, and eventually impart it into other substances.

We are going to start by teaching you how to perceive your own energy field. This invisible field is around us constantly, and it extends out from the physical body about one to two inches, depending on the person. If you are able to see auras, this is the "empty" space or gap between the body and where the aura begins. One simple way to begin sensing your own energy immediately is this: Hold your hands palms up and facing each other, and bring your palms closer together until they are about an inch apart. At this point, you should be able to feel energy. To me, it feels like putting two magnets together; my hands seem attracted to each other and I feel like they are tugging at me to close the gap between them. For other people, it may seem like two repelling magnets are keeping your hands apart.

An energy center, or *chakra*, is located in the palm of each hand. There are seven major chakras aligned in a straight line down the center of the body, starting at the crown and ending at the groin, while numerous minor chakras are spread throughout the body. We'll work with the major chakras in subsequent exercises. For the first exercise, we are going to focus on the minor chakras in the palms of your hands.

You can do most of the exercises in this chapter alone, but the final one is designed for use with a partner. The exercises build upon each other and are arranged from the easiest to the more challenging. Some might seem silly or simplistic, but I would ask that you don't skip them.

EXERCISE 2.1

Sensing your own energy

For this exercise you will need:

Five to ten minutes
Soap and water
A towel

In this exercise, you will learn how to access your own personal energy at the palm chakras. This technique is the basic building block for the other exercises in this chapter and for the spells in later chapters. It's very important that you know how to do it correctly before you move on. I would recommend practicing it several times.

First, cleanse your hands with soap and water, paying close attention to the palms. You'll want to take a couple minutes to do so, then dry your hands on the towel. You can do this in the bathroom or kitchen sink.

Once your hands are cleansed and dried, find a comfortable place where you won't be disturbed and take a few moments to get centered. Now bring the palms of your hands together, and rub them against each other or clap your hands until you start to feel the chakras open. This can be a feeling of warmth, tingling, or coldness in the center of your palms. My great-grandmother did this before she started any magical working.

When you feel that your chakras are open, hold your hands about an inch apart. You should feel a mild "magnetized" sensation between your hands, like they want to come together. Got it? Good.

Each of us has a dominant hand; this is the hand where we give energy. For most of us, this is the one we write with. We also have a passive hand; this is where we receive energy. With your dominant hand, fold your fingers so they are resting against the fleshy part of your hand, but aren't touching your palm. Stick your thumb out. You should look almost like you're trying to hitch a ride, but don't make a fist; you don't want to block your chakra.

Now hold your non-dominant hand palm up. Move your dominant hand so your thumb is parallel to your open palm, about an inch or so above it. Your thumb should not touch your palm at all. Starting at the edge of your wrist, move your dominant hand in a sweeping motion toward the tips of the fingers on your non-dominant hand. What do you feel?

Ideally, you should be able to sense a variation in the energy coming from your non-dominant hand. There should be more sensation when your thumb goes over your open palm chakra than when it goes over your wrist or fingers. If you didn't feel a difference, try it again, but this time, move your dominant hand down your wrist to your elbow, then back to the palm. Be aware of the various sensations you experience; as I said, some people perceive energy as a tingle, others as heat. Also, the sensations may be very slight to start with. This is why you need to practice the exercise until you are familiar with the way you, personally, sense energy.

Working with the chakras is very powerful. It allows us to increase the energy directed into our spells, which in turn increases the effectiveness of the spell itself. The chakras are natural "doorways" for energy to enter and exit our bodies. The latent energy that exists within us and around us is amplified at the chakras, and they serve as the best place to store raised energy and to direct energy from. In much of the spellwork you'll learn here, we'll use the hand chakras to raise energy and to direct the energy into objects. We'll also utilize the major chakras to raise energy from the earth and channel it to the hand chakras for a particular use.

Each living being on the earth has its own energy field, and so do inanimate objects. Even rocks and trees have energy, since they are part of the earth. In natural or folk magick we call this energy the "spirit" of these beings, and each creature or object is "in tune" to a particular kind of energy. For example, jasmine corresponds to love, and so does rose quartz. If we wanted to do a love spell, we might want to incorporate these elements in some way. There are many excellent books available that discuss correspondences; see the recommended reading list for more information. Meanwhile, our next exercise deals with sensing energy around various types of objects.

EXERCISE 2.2

The energy of inanimate objects

For this exercise you will need:

> *Five to fifteen minutes*
> *A rock—any type will do, as long as it's not quartz or a crystal*
> *An apple, orange, banana, pear or other type of whole fruit*
> *A green leaf*
> *A crystal or a piece of quartz*

Arrange the above items on a table or flat surface, an equal distance apart. Begin by opening up your hand chakras, then form your dominant hand into the shape outlined in exercise 2.1—thumb extended and fingers bent. We'll refer to this shape as the thumb-out position.

Start with the rock. Leave it on the table and hold your palm above it, about a half-inch from touching it directly. Move your palm in a sweeping motion around the contours of the rock, making sure that your hand is always about a half-inch away and that you are not touching the rock itself at all. What do you feel?

After the rock, move on to the fruit, the leaf, and finally the crystal, repeating the same procedure. Do you feel a difference in the energy from one item to the next? Is the energy stronger or easier to feel in one item as compared to the others?

For the second part of this exercise, you'll want to begin by clearing the energy from your hand chakras. To do that, rub your hands together in a circular motion. This will dispel the built-up energy from the first part of the exercise without closing your chakras.

Again, start with the rock. This time, pick it up and place it in the palm of your receiving hand. Form your dominant hand into the thumb-out position and hold it above the rock. Make sure to keep your palm directly above the rock, about a half-inch away. In a sweeping motion, move your palm over the contours of the rock, making sure that you don't touch it or your receiving hand. Does the energy feel different from before? Is it stronger or weaker?

Once you are done with the rock, repeat the exercise with the other objects. Does their energy feel different from before? Stronger or weaker?

I chose the items for the above exercise because there are clear differences in their energy. To me, the rock seems to hum quietly with energy; it feels very stable and immutable. An apple has a more delicate energy. It resonates slowly and feels as if the energy within it is dissipating or disappearing as it is transformed into food for the seeds inside it. The leaf has a more shocking energy; it feels like a jolt of static electricity. It throbs with energy, giving its all and holding nothing back. And the crystal has the strongest energy of them all; it sings with the force of its energy. Its vibration is dramatically increased when it comes into contact with the energy in the palm chakra of my receiving hand, almost as if it is tuning itself to my frequency.

Your results may or may not be similar to mine. Each person senses energy differently and each person relates to various objects in his or her own unique way. I'm sharing my own experience to help you understand the exercise, not to give you the "definitive" reaction to the energy of these objects. I hope that you were able to feel something in this exercise; if not, try again on a different day, at a different time of day, or in a different location. Some trial and error may be necessary.

I encourage you to practice this exercise several times with other types of objects; doing so will really help you understand how you sense energy. It will also give you a frame of reference for how the energy of various objects should feel, which will come in handy later on when you may encounter energy that doesn't feel "right."

EXERCISE 2.3

Cycling internal energy

For this exercise you will need:

> *Fifteen to twenty minutes*
> *A comfortable place to sit or lie down*

Up to this point, we have been working only with the minor energy centers in the palms of the hands. In this exercise, we will learn how to open up and cycle energy through the seven major chakras, which are arranged in a line down the length of the spine. This important exercise will introduce you to directing energy, which will be essential in later exercises and in the spells presented in later chapters.

Sit or lie down someplace comfortable where you will not be disturbed. Take a couple minutes to relax, releasing the tension from all parts of your body, starting with your feet, moving through each part of the body, and finishing with your head and face. Focus on areas that feel tense or uncomfortable and consciously relax them. Keep going until you are completely relaxed, but not so relaxed that you fall asleep!

Start by directing your attention to your crown, the area at the very top of your head. This is the location of the first chakra. In your mind's eye, picture this energy center as a spinning disk of violet light. Feel the chakra open. You might feel warmth or a tingling sensation. Take a minute or so to focus on the feeling of having your crown chakra open. Recognize how it feels. Sense the latent energy there.

When you are ready to move on, focus your attention on your third eye, the area on your brow between your eyes. This is the location of the second chakra. In your mind's eye, picture a spinning disk of indigo-colored energy. Feel the chakra open and enjoy the sensation. Take a minute or so to focus on this chakra, on the way the latent energy feels at your third eye.

Next, move your attention to your throat—the area at the base of your neck. This is the location of your third chakra, which is associated with energy of bright, clear blue. Take a couple moments to focus on this energy center. Visualize it opening and note the sensation before moving on.

The fourth energy center is located in the center of your rib cage at your heart. Focus on that chakra now and visualize a spinning disk of pure green energy. Feel the chakra opening and feel the sensation of the energy moving. Again, take a moment to focus on the way it feels before moving on.

Next, move your attention to your solar plexus, the area right at the top of your stomach. This is the location of the fifth chakra, and it vibrates to the color yellow. Feel this energy center open. Feel the sensation of the energy moving through this area. Make sure you understand the way it feels before moving on.

The sixth chakra is located about midway down your stomach, behind your navel. Visualize a spinning disk of orange energy, and concentrate on feeling the energy center open. Take a moment to focus on the energy there, to become familiar with how it feels.

Finally, we reach the seventh or root chakra, which is located at the base of your spine. It is associated with the color red. Concentrate on feeling this energy center open. Take a moment to sense its latent energy and note how it feels.

Now that all your chakras are open, focus on all seven of them together. Feel the connection that runs between each energy center down the center of your body. Realize that even though the energy centers are separate, the energy is not static—it moves between all the chakras. As your latent energy moves between the chakras, it is transformed and takes on the characteristics of the chakra where it is centered, until it moves on. Feel how the energy is slightly different at each energy center and take several moments to meditate on the differences.

When you are ready, place your dominant hand on your crown chakra. Feel the energy pulse between your hand and your crown, then as you remove your hand, feel the chakra return to its natural dormant state. Repeat this process with each of the remaining chakras.

When you feel you're done with this exercise, sit up if you've been lying down, open your eyes if they've been closed, and return your attention to the world around you. You might want to rub your hands together to dispel any residual energy.

Focusing on the chakras allows us to feel the latent energy that is constantly around us. It also allows us to connect to the latent energy in other objects, like the items we used in exercise 2.2. This force is all around us and within us at all times, and it doesn't require any additional work to have access to it. This is referred to as personal energy—the energy that you need to live. However, this is not the energy that you will use for spells. That force comes from the universe around us; we draw it in, combine it with our personal energy, and then direct it to attain the goals of our spells.

Using only personal energy in spells is not a good idea. It can be done, but it leaves you drained, and you then have to replenish your personal energy, which takes time and effort. On the other hand, working with universal energy, which is infinite, has the opposite effect—it leaves you rejuvenated. Sometimes it also leaves you with an excess amount of energy that must be returned to the universe, since it can be overwhelming to your energy centers. Having too much energy is like having a really bad caffeine high. The best way to return this energy is to ground, and we'll get to that in chapter three, right after we get to the part where we will learn how to access or raise the universal energy.

The following exercises will teach you to connect with the energy of the earth, other beings around you, and the universe. Learning to make these connections will be essential to the success of your spells; this is one of the fundamental building blocks of successful magical workings. Connecting to the vast energy of the earth allows you to add extra energy to your spells, and connecting to the people around you allows you to cast spells that help others and work effectively in a group setting. (If you're a new witch, it might seem inconceivable that you might someday want to work with others, but I assure you it's a strong possibility.) It's important to be able to sense the energy of other people as well as to connect to it; more on that later.

Earth energy is all around us. It's easy to feel it when you're alone in a beautiful place on a sunny day. It's not so easy to feel it when you're rushing around trying to get to work or school, when you hardly have a moment to notice the sun, much less to revel in its warmth. We draw so much of our energy from the world around us, but most of us don't really connect with the earth unless we are in circle or working on a spell. But the earth is always there, waiting.

The first time I really connected with the earth was on a spring day when I was ten. My grandmother had sent me to buy eggs from the Bedouin tribe that lived just outside our town in the Jordan Valley. Going to the Bedouin camp always felt like stepping back in time. They still lived in camel hair tents. They made their money by selling eggs, cheese, yogurt, butter, and occasionally meat to their neighbors. I never knew if they lived that way by choice or necessity. On one hand, I envied them a life of such simplicity; on the other hand, I was too much a city girl to live without running water or electricity.

After getting the eggs that day, I decided to take a short-cut home that my cousin had told me about, instead of heading back the way I'd come. I got a little lost. The Jordan Valley is the lowest place on earth at about three hundred feet below sea level. I came across a little red rock gorge that I'm sure is the absolute lowest place on earth, as well as one of the loveliest. The closest approximation I've found here in the States is the red rock formations I saw on a road trip through Sedona, Arizona. That isolated ravine was incredibly peaceful, with a stillness that I found so comforting. Think about your own experiences. Have you encountered a place that radiated earth energy?

EXERCISE 2.4

Earth energy

For this exercise you will need:

Fifteen to thirty minutes, ideally early in the morning when there are few people around

In this exercise, you will learn to recognize the energy of the earth itself. To do so, you must get outside. Your backyard will do, if you have one. Urban witches may need to visit a local park or hiking trail.

Take five to ten minutes and simply walk around the area. Listen to the birdsong; look for small animals darting along. See the trees around you, so firmly rooted into the ground. Feel the sun on your face and the breeze caressing your hair. Feel your breath as you exhale; if it is cold enough, you can see it meld with the universe. This place is serene and every step brings you closer to the same serenity you feel surrounding you. Enjoy that feeling. Nature is all around; you are surrounded by its energy. You can feel it seeping in through your pores, coming in with the air you inhale. To me, this feeling is bliss. Can you sense the energy? How does it feel to you?

When you're ready, find a secluded, comfortable place to sit down. Sit on the earth, in the grass, in the sand on the beach, with your back against a tree—anywhere you like, as long as you are on the ground rather than a bench or other structure. If you can, sit cross-legged with your hands resting palms up on your thighs. Keep your back erect, so that you are sitting as closely as possible to the lotus position. This aligns your major chakras.

Close your eyes and focus for a moment on relaxing your body, releasing any accumulated tension. Breathe deeply, inhaling relaxation and exhaling the tension from your body until you feel completely relaxed. At that point, start opening your chakras as detailed in the previous exercise. Start with the crown and move down to the root chakra.

When all seven of your energy centers are open and connected, focus again on your root chakra. In the cross-legged position, this chakra is closest to the earth. From it, visualize tendrils of your energy extending like roots into the earth below you. These roots go down into the ground seeking the energy core of the earth, which supplies infinite energy to all those able to connect to it. Visualize your roots going down through the bedrock, deep into the center of the earth, until they connect to the energy source there. Feel this energy as your roots connect to it; see it as a river of pure white light in your mind's eye. This river flows beneath the solid surface of the earth and can be accessed at any time. Plunge your roots into the flowing energy river; feel the energy swirling around them. Notice that your roots, though separate from the energy river, are made from the same substance. As you realize this, your roots begin to merge with the earth energy until they are one, and you can no longer tell where your roots end and the earth energy begins.

Now take a moment and focus on how that feels. Sense the infinite nature of the energy you are connected to and how it is identical in many ways to your own personal energy. This is the eternal earth; it will be here long after the body you occupy has turned to dust. The perceived separation between you and the earth is artificial, finite, and temporary, because you and it are made of the same essence. Take several minutes to enjoy the connection between yourself and the earth.

When you are ready, say goodbye to Mother Earth and feel your roots slowly separate themselves from the energy river. Feel them re-form, whole and complete, still submerged in the energy river. Then begin slowly to pull them

back through the earth. Feel them retract until they recon-
nect with the chakra at the base of your spine and merge
again with your personal energy. Focus now on each of
your chakras, starting with the root and moving upward
to the crown. Return them to their natural dormant condition. As you do so, you realize that you feel energized,
like you've had eight restful hours of sleep. When you are
ready, open your eyes.

This is one of my favorite exercises. Afterward, I always
feel refreshed and connected to the earth and the world
around me. The purpose of the exercise is to introduce
you to the energy of the earth, and to instruct you in how
to connect with it. In chapter three, you'll learn how to
draw that same energy upward and then direct it outward
from your energy centers into animate or inanimate objects to add energy to your spells. Ideally, energy will act
like the "battery" for your spell—the infinite resource that
works with your intent and your continual positive reinforcement to produce the results you desire.

Next, we'll move on to learning to connect with the energy of other living beings such as plants and animals.

Plant and animal energy

For this exercise you will need:

> *Ten to fifteen minutes*
> *A domesticated pet that is comfortable in your presence*
> *A living plant or tree*

We will go through this exercise in two ways, first with a pet and then with a living tree or plant. Please do both sections, as the exercise is designed to give you a wider frame of reference for sensing differences in the energy of various types of living things.

A cat or dog you have good relationship with would be best for this exercise, but any domestic animal that will stay still for a short amount of time and remain docile would also work. The last thing I want is for you to injure yourself or your pet by doing this exercise. That defeats the purpose of what we are attempting to do and the connection we're trying to establish.

Part A: Animal

As always, choose a comfortable place where you won't be disturbed. Take a couple moments to stroke and pet the animal you'll be connecting with. Make sure that he or she is comfortable, secure, and relaxed. While continuing to stroke and pet your animal, begin the process of centering yourself. Breathe deeply and release the tension in your body until you are completely relaxed.

When you feel ready, stop stroking your pet for a moment and open your hand chakras by rubbing or gently clapping them together as explained in exercise 2.1. Try not to startle your pet with loud noises as you do so.

Place your hands over your pet, palm down, about a foot apart, and four or five inches above his or her fur or skin. You should not be touching the animal at this point. Move your hands slightly up and down until you sense the edge of his or her energy field. This is usually found about four to six inches away from the surface of the fur or skin, but it can be closer or farther away depending on the usual energy level of your animal. A high-strung pet will usually have a larger energy field than a calmer animal; of course, there are individual exceptions to this.

The energy field will feel warm on the open chakras of your palms. You might also feel a tingling sensation or a vibration. Don't feel bad if you have to try several times before finding the edge of the energy field. The first time I tried to do this, it took ten attempts before I found the correct distance. It's important to get this right, so if you are in doubt, keeping trying. It may help if you close your eyes, especially at first. Each time, move your hands inward and then upward. If you are within the right distance, moving your hands inward should feel like sinking into warmth; the tingle should increase or the vibrations will feel more intense. As you pull your hands away, there will be a sensation of coldness or distance. For this exercise, you want to identify the edge of the energy field, where you can feel the energy but where your hands are not submerged in it. When you have found the right place, take a couple moments to sense how this energy feels under your hands.

Now draw back your hands until you are one or two inches away from the edge of the energy field. As we did in the last exercise, extend tendrils of energy outward, this time from the open chakras in your palms. Your personal energy should just touch the energy of your animal, but should not penetrate his or her energy field. Brush the tendrils of your energy lightly over the energy field of your pet, almost as if you are petting him or her.

Then, very slowly and gently, extend the tendrils of your energy into his or her energy field. Don't be surprised if your pet jumps or is startled by this. If that happens, stop and try the exercise again later. Depending on how sensitive your animal is, it might take several tries to train him or her to accept this intrusion into his or her personal space.

Once you've gotten your pet to lie still and be comfortable with the process, begin merging your energy with his or her energy, like we did with the earth energy in the last exercise. Take a couple moments to focus on how all the energy feels. Remember that your energy and your pet's energy come from the same source, and that it is a finite version of the earth energy you connected to in the last exercise.

When you are ready, begin to separate your energy from that of your pet. Slowly and gently withdraw your energy tendrils until once again they are just brushing the edges of the animal's energy field. Let the tendrils rest there for a moment, and again stroke them lightly over the energy field of your pet, almost as if you are petting him or her. Then withdraw them completely, back into the open chakras in your palms. Make sure that you are only taking back your own energy and aren't taking anything from your pet as you do this. Return the palm chakras to their natural dormant state, and take a few minutes to stroke and comfort your pet. How did the exercise feel?

Part B: Plant

For this part of the exercise, you can use a healthy living tree or plant that is in the ground, or a potted plant as long as it is healthy and well developed. A plant that has just been planted or transplanted is not the best subject for this exercise, because its energy will be in a state of flux and will be harder to sense and connect to.

If you are using a potted plant, feel free to move it to a comfortable place where you will be undisturbed. If you are working with a tree or a plant rooted in the ground, do the best you can to get comfortable. Take a couple minutes to breathe deeply in and out, consciously relaxing and releasing all the tension from your body.

When you feel ready, open your palm chakras by rubbing or clapping your hands together. Hold your hands, palms in, near the trunk of the tree or the main stem of the plant, and away from the leaves. Start with your hands about three to four inches away from the plant, not touching it at all. Move your hands back and forth and try to sense the edge of the plant's energy field. If you are working with a tree, you might have to move back a foot or so to find the edge of the field, particularly if the tree is really old. If you are using a potted plant, you may have to move your hands inward until they are barely an inch away from the stem of the plant. The size of the energy field will vary based on the size of the plant or tree, as well as its age.

The energy field will feel warm on your open palm chakras; you might also feel a tingling sensation or a vibration when you get to its edge. Again, don't get discouraged if you have to try several times. This is normal, especially considering that plant energy is more subtle than that of an animal. It's important to get this right, so if you are in doubt, keep experimenting. Try it with your eyes closed as well as open. Move your hands inward and then upward. If you are within the correct distance, moving your hands inward should feel like sinking into warmth, with increased tingling or more intense vibrations. As you move your hands away, there will be a sensation of coldness or distance. Try to locate the edge of the energy field, where you can sense the energy but where your hands are not submerged in it. When you have found the right place, take a couple moments to sense how this energy feels under your hands. Make sure that you are very aware of how this energy feels to you.

Now move your hands farther away, until you are one or two inches away from the edge of the plant's energy field. Just as we did in part A of this exercise, extend tendrils of energy from your open palm chakras outward until they touch the energy field. Your personal energy should just touch the energy of the plant, but should not penetrate it. Just brush the tendrils of your energy lightly over that of the plant, almost as if you are caressing it.

Very slowly and gently, extend the tendrils of your energy into the energy field of the plant, until the tendrils are completely submerged. Obviously you won't get a reaction here, as you may have with your pet. Begin the process of merging your energy with that of the plant, and take a few minutes to focus on how it feels. Keep in mind that both your energy and the plant's come from the same source, the infinite earth energy you connected to in exercise 2.4.

When you feel ready, begin to separate your energy from that of the plant. Slowly and gently withdraw your energy tendrils until once again they are just brushing the edges of the energy field. Let the tendrils rest there for a moment, and then withdraw them completely into the open chakras in your palms. Make sure that you are only taking back your own energy and aren't taking anything from the plant as you do this. Return the palm chakras to their natural dormant state. How did this exercise feel? How was it similar to what you experienced in part A? How did it differ?

It is very important to be aware of the possible ramifications of connecting to, or interfering with, the energy of living beings, because this skill can be used in both positive and negative ways. While taking away energy from a plant or an animal can have harmful effects, doing the same to an individual is considered psychic vampirism, and is a very negative and immoral use of your abilities. (If you need additional energy, you can take it from the earth; she willingly and endlessly gives of her energy to her children.) However, a *conscious* exchange of energy between willing individuals is possible and can be a very positive experience. The goal of the next exercise is to combine energy with a partner, but without giving or taking energy (purposefully or inadvertently).

Any agreement to exchange energy should be entered into willingly by both parties, whether in the form of this exercise or when doing any sort of energy work or casting a spell on or for an individual. Please keep in mind that doing energy work on or for a person without his or her knowledge and permission is manipulative; it strips away a person's free will and it might deprive him or her of a needed lesson. Although it is sometimes tempting to do a working because it will be "good for" that person, it is not your place to decide what is good for another individual. That is the job of the divine, the higher self, and the individual. How would you feel if someone took away *your* free will? Interfering with a person's free will is something that you want to avoid at all costs; the karmic penalties are huge, and just not worth it.

All the spells I teach here involve changing the energy around yourself to attain your desired goals, and only two exercises involve an energy exchange with an individual (or individuals) without explicit consent. For now, a good rule of thumb to establish, particularly if you are a new witch, is: *no spells for unwilling people.* An unwilling person is *anyone who did not give you an express verbal agreement to cast a spell for him or her.* Even in the case where a person asks for your help with a spell, you should always ask yourself, "Is this something I want to be involved in?"

I know that some of you who are reading this are thinking, "I can do whatever I want." True, you can. I don't expect, just because you're reading this book, that you are

Wiccan and follow the Rede, but I do expect that you will swiftly become aware of the consequences of your actions. Remember, like is attracted to like. If you don't want someone to do it to you, don't do it to someone else.

Connecting to the energy of other people is important in group spells. Sensing the energy of others is doubly important because you don't want to connect with or work with people whose energy is negative or whose goals don't conform to your own. That doesn't mean that you shouldn't help people who are surrounded by negative energy, but you must be very cautious when doing so. Negativity is contagious; it is like a black hole that can suck you in if you aren't careful.

In chapter 1, we talked about how sending out negative thoughts and energy can actually cancel out your spellwork or produce results that are contrary to the stated goals of the spell. Negativity around a person can act in the same way: have you ever met someone who tends to have bad luck, and not coincidentally has a bad attitude? This is a perfect example of the principle "like attracts like." This doesn't necessarily mean that someone who is surrounded by negativity is a bad person or has done bad things. While it's true that negativity around a person can come from his or her own destructive or hurtful actions, it can also come from self-defeating thoughts and low self-esteem, or by absorbing the negativity of others.

The latter can also be true of buildings and other physical locations, which often hold the residue of the negativity of the people who live there or used to live there. If you've ever experienced "bad vibes" walking into a place, you've sensed negativity intuitively.

Many people get stuck in their own negativity and find themselves unable to get out. Negativity is self-perpetuating; like a fire it consumes everything around it, growing exponentially stronger as more energy is created through each negative occurrence. It takes a gigantic effort of will to redirect all that bad energy toward thinking and acting more positively, but part of being a witch is recognizing patterns like this and learning how to break them. Spells can help, as can ritual cleansings of the home and workplace. But these tools are only part of what is needed to break the cycle. We discussed earlier that spells require a commitment to stay "on message" to work; our lives are the same way. For positive things to happen to us, we need to create a positive environment, not just physically, but mentally.

A large part of being a successful witch is having a positive attitude. This mindset does three things for us. First, it gives confidence, which is translated into other parts of our life. Think about the really successful people you know. Do they constantly radiate negativity? Probably not. Secondly, being positive it makes it easier to stay "on message," in our spellwork and in everyday life. Lastly, it just makes you feel better. It's amazing how much more energetic, spontaneous, and alive you feel when you are not constantly dragged down by doubt and negativity. Our thoughts (and, to a lesser extent, the thoughts of others) are constantly altering the energy field surrounding us, positively or negatively. This is one reason teachers of magick often insist on secrecy. It has nothing to do with shame; it is to minimize the interference of external energy that can change or negate an anticipated result.

It takes a great deal of practice to help others deal with their negativity and to help them eliminate it from their lives, while at the same time preventing that negative energy from becoming attached to you. A person surrounded by negativity is seldom completely innocent of contributing to this condition; he or she must be willing to do the work needed to change or any energy you put into helping him or her will be worthless. Remember, your first responsibility is to yourself; only when you have yourself and your own issues under control can you help others.

As witches, we are often asked for help; this is an important part of our calling. It is a way of giving back positive things to the world. Especially at first, we may have the idea that, since magick has done so much for us, we can use it to do much for others. That is true, and it's a great feeling to be able to help people. However, before stepping in, you should always ask yourself, "Is this something or someone I want to be involved with?"

This is also a question to consider when choosing your partner for the next exercise. It is essential to choose a person surrounded by positive rather than negative energy—someone you trust, someone you feel safe letting down your defenses with. Most of us learned early in life how to differentiate positive from negative energy—after all, who wants to be around someone who constantly whines or complains? Wouldn't you rather be around someone who is cheerful, with a good attitude? There's a tangible difference between positive and negative energy, and we'll explore it more, later on.

Connecting with the energy of another individual can be a very powerful and moving experience, much more so than when you connected with the energy of the earth, your pet, and a plant. This connection is, in some ways, more intimate than sex. You will be working with an active rather than a passive sentience, where barriers can be actively dropped by both sides for increased results, and the amount and vibration of energy that you will be connecting to will be higher than anything we have explored thus far.

The first step in achieving an energetic connection with another person is to lower one's natural barriers. This is not as difficult as it may sound and it requires no prior experience working with energy. As living beings, we are constantly fielding a barrage of stimuli, and we learn early on how to tune out things that are not directly related to us. We do this to survive, because if we had to pay attention to everything going on at once, we would quickly be overwhelmed. Similarly, we tune out much of the energy around us, including that which comes from other people. These are our natural barriers or defenses. They are created automatically, without conscious thought or effort, and of course some individuals' defenses are stronger than others. Some people believe that "gaps" in these barriers enable psychic phenomena; if you can develop a methodology for selectively lowering portions of your barriers, you may have better access to precognition, past life memories, and overall psychic abilities. For now, it's enough that you understand what barriers are and learn how to lower them.

It's not necessary to lower all your barriers in this exercise. If you think of your natural defenses as being like layers of clothing, you'll be taking off your jacket but will otherwise be fully clothed. Our goal is to create a *selective* gap that allows you to connect to and merge with the energy of your partner. This exercise will teach you how to do just that.

Connecting with a partner

For this exercise you will need:

A human partner

Thirty to forty-five minutes

A comfortable, quiet place where you won't be disturbed

This exercise is the most complex one of this chapter; however, it is the most interesting and rewarding one, too. It's designed in two parts, based on the characteristics of your chosen partner. You can work through both parts, or just the one most applicable to your situation. Part A is intended for those with partners who have no prior experience working with energy or who are not interested in actively participating in the exercise, and so will be passive recipients. Part B is designed for people with partners who are either experienced with energy work or who are also working through this book. If you intend to do both parts of the exercise, begin with part A. The steps you will take in lowering your barriers are the same for both parts of the exercise, and should be done by both participants.

For this exercise to be successful, it's important that you try to leave behind any unresolved issues you might have with your partner. Unresolved anger in particular can make it difficult to lower one's barriers, which is an essential part of the exercise.

Lowering your barriers

Begin by sitting in a comfortable position, preferably on the ground, facing your partner. Close your eyes and breathe deeply, inhaling relaxation and exhaling any tension from your body. Take a couple moments to breathe in and out, just making sure that you are completely at ease. When you feel ready, focus on the breathing of your partner. Try to match your breathing to that of your partner, breathing in as he breathes out, breathing out as he breathes in. Take several moments to get used to breathing in harmony without any obvious effort. Don't try to force it; just relax and let it come naturally.

In your mind's eye, picture the energy field around your body. Feel it emanating from you, surrounding you with energy (it may help to close your eyes as you tune in). As you do this, you may feel a tingling sensation, or a feeling of warmth or coldness around you. This is the way your body attempts to communicate its perception of your energy field. Continue to breathe in harmony with your partner. Once you have the energy field fixed in your mind's eye, begin to push your perception to its edge. At the edge of your field, you sense a solid barrier, which prevents your energy from mixing with that of your partner. You don't want to eliminate this barrier; instead, you want to make it porous, so that you can allow energy to pass in and out of it. Visualize tiny pores in this shield that filter out 99 percent of the energy around you. Think of the pores as gate-keepers; they only admit the energy you choose and deflect everything else. Hold that command firmly in your mind as you create the pores. Only the energy you allow will enter; all other energy will be deflected.

Part A: Working with a passive partner

At this point, the passive partner should focus on his or her breathing and concentrate on keeping open the pores in his or her barrier.

Once you have created the pores within your own barrier, begin focusing on your own energy field and that of your partner. Using the technique learned in exercise 2.4, send tendrils of energy from your root chakra deep into the earth. But this time, rather than simply merging your energy with that of the earth, begin to pull the earth energy upward, through the tendrils and into your root chakra. Push this energy upward through each of the chakras until you reach your crown chakra.

Take a moment and focus on the energy flowing up through the earth and moving through each of your chakras, up from your root and onward to your crown. Feel this energy pulsate at each of your major energy centers. Each time the energy pulses, it expands, growing larger, and the distance between your chakras grows smaller and smaller. Finally, the amount of energy at each chakra is enough that the centers are touching, merging. The energy becomes a river rather than small pools. The energy river rushes through your chakras and begins to expand your energy field outward. Feel the energy expand around you, extending to brush against the energy field of your partner. Once you sense that the energy fields are touching, stop pulling up energy from the earth, but don't withdraw your tendrils. Continue to hold the energy you have, keeping it moving through your chakras so it doesn't become stagnant.

Once the two fields are touching, notice that your own energy field is much larger than your partner's. Begin to merge your energy into the energy field of your partner, through the open pores in his barrier. As you do so, feel his energy field expand and your own energy field contract until both are roughly the same size. Take a couple moments to focus on any sensations you may experience. Can you distinguish between your energy and that of your partner? Notice the similarities and the differences.

When you're ready, direct your energy as we did in exercises 2.4 and 2.5 and begin pulling it back—out of your partner's energy field, through his barrier, through your own barrier. Make sure that you withdraw only your own energy, taking none of his, and also that you leave none of your own behind. Go back to the point where your energy fields are touching, but the energy is not mixing.

Next, you will return the energy you pulled up back to the earth. To do so, focus on your own energy field, noticing that it is much larger than usual, just as it was before you merged with your partner. Visualize your energy field returning to its normal size as you take the excess energy and direct it into your crown chakra, then down through your major energy centers to your root chakra. Feel the energy centers returning to their normal size as the energy flows downward. From your root chakra, send the excess energy through your tendrils and back into the earth. Make sure you return only the energy that you brought up and none of your own. When all the excess energy has been returned, withdraw your energy tendrils from the earth and bring them up to merge into your root chakra.

This final step should be done by both partners. Focus on your own energy field and direct your attention to its very edge, where you created the pores in its barrier. Take a moment to locate the pores and feel them. Then, in your mind's eye, visualize the pores closing (but they are still there and can be opened by you at any time). When you're ready, open your eyes if they've been closed, and return to normal consciousness. You feel refreshed, like you've had a good night's sleep.

I recommend discussing your experiences with your partner. How were your perceptions and physical sensations similar? How were they different? Do you feel closer to your partner now than before the exercise? Did any new insights about him or her occur to you?

Part B: Working with an active partner

After following the above directions for lowering your barriers, you and your partner should each focus on your own energy field. Using the technique learned in exercise 2.4, send tendrils of energy from your root chakra deep into the earth. But this time, rather than simply merging your energy with that of the earth, begin to pull the earth energy upward, through the tendrils and into your root chakra. Push this energy upward through each of the chakras until you reach your crown chakra.

Take a moment and focus on the energy flowing up through the earth and moving through each of your chakras, up from your root and onward to your crown. Feel this energy pulsate at each of your major energy centers. Each time the energy pulses, it expands, growing larger, and the distance between your chakras grows smaller and smaller. Finally, the amount of energy at each chakra is enough that the centers are touching, merging. The energy becomes a river rather than small pools. The energy river rushes through your chakras and begins to expand your energy field outward. Feel the energy expand around you, extending to brush against the energy field of your partner. Once you sense that the energy fields are touching, stop pulling up energy from the earth, but don't withdraw your tendrils. Continue to hold the energy you have, keeping it moving through your chakras so it doesn't become stagnant.

Once the two energy fields are touching, begin extending the energy you've pulled up into the energy field of your partner, through the open pores in his or her barrier. Your partner should do the same to you. Both partners are directing their own energy into each other's fields and are receiving energy in return—a reciprocal exchange of energy. Take a couple moments to focus on any sensations you may experience. Can you distinguish between your energy and that of your partner? Notice the similarities and the differences.

When you're ready, direct your energy as we did in exercises 2.4 and 2.5 and begin pulling it back—out of your partner's energy field, through his barrier, through your own barrier. Make sure that you withdraw only your own energy, taking none of his, and also that you leave none of your own behind. Go back to the point where your energy fields are touching, but the energy is not mixing.

Next, each of you will return the energy you pulled up back to the earth. To do so, focus on your own energy field, noticing that it is much larger than usual, just as it was before you merged with your partner. Visualize your energy field returning to its normal size as you take the excess energy and direct it into your crown chakra, then down through your major energy centers to your root chakra. Feel the energy centers returning to their normal size as the energy flows downward. From your root chakra, send the excess energy through your tendrils and back into the earth. Make sure you return only the energy that you brought up and none of your own. When all the excess energy has been returned, withdraw your energy tendrils from the earth and bring them up to merge into your root chakra.

Finally, each of you will focus on your own energy field. Direct your attention to its very edge, where you created the pores in its barrier. Take a moment to locate the pores and feel them. Then, in your mind's eye, visualize the pores closing (but they are still there and can be opened by you at any time). When you're ready, open your eyes if they've been closed, and return to normal consciousness. You feel refreshed, like you've had a good night's sleep.

Once again, I recommend discussing your experiences with your partner. How were your perceptions and physical sensations similar? How were they different? Do you feel closer to your partner now than before the exercise? Did any new insights about him or her occur to you? If you did part A, how does working with an active partner differ from working with a passive one?

There are some very practical applications for this exercise, particularly in group spellwork and healing. For that reason, it's important that you practice the techniques until you feel proficient. It's better for you to go slowly and make sure that you learn everything in a way that works for you, rather than rushing through the book and then expecting to know everything.

The final exercise of this chapter is designed to teach you how to sense negative energy around you. We won't connect with this energy directly, of course, but we'll take what we learned from exercise 2.6 and apply it in a different way to sense the energy that surrounds individuals. This will also enable you to sense negativity around a particular location or situation. This simple technique is something you should get in the habit of doing whenever you feel that you've come into contact with negative or undesirable energy, and any time you do magical work with someone you aren't familiar with or comfortable with.

When you are a member of a coven or group, you don't always have a choice of whom you work with, particularly in an open ritual setting; you don't get to pick who shows up and what their intent is. But if the working is to be successful, it requires merging your energy with everyone else's. Just as we can come into contact with unsavory or depressed people in our mundane lives, so too can we encounter these people in circle, and we don't want to carry their energy around with us. Thus we need to learn to clear unwanted energy from our own energy field. This is the first exercise we have done that adds the element of intent.

EXERCISE 2.7

Clearing negative energy

For this exercise you will need:

Ten minutes

A quiet place where you won't be disturbed

Sit comfortably, either cross-legged on the floor or in a straight-backed chair that allows you to keep your spine straight. Go through the steps of exercise 2.3 to open up your major chakras.

In your mind's eye, see your own energy field as beautiful, clear blue light. Within this blue light, and starting with your crown chakra, look for the presence of any energy that doesn't match your own. This energy may present itself visually as black spots or cloudy areas, or it may feel heavy and stagnant. This isn't necessarily "bad" energy; it is just energy that you don't want or need mixed in with yours. Here we add the element of intent: your intent is to rid yourself of that energy. Gather it all into a little ball. Move on to inspect each of your major chakras, adding any negativity you may find to the ball and directing it downward until you reach your root chakra.

Once you've collected everything you want to get rid of, direct the ball of energy out through the base of your root chakra and into the ground. Push this energy down until it merges with the earth. Watch it dissolve back into the primal energy of the earth until you can no longer sense it or distinguish it. Then focus on your energy field and the barrier at its edge. Remember all those tiny pores? Make sure they're closed, sealing your own energy in and all negativity out. Take a moment to return each of your chakras to its usual dormant state. When you feel ready, open your eyes.

I try to do this exercise every morning, particularly if I'm working in a stressful environment or with people that I find particularly negative. When I'm not under a lot of stress or when I'm not around negativity and negative people, I only need to do this once or twice a month. You will learn what works best for you. I also recommend doing it whenever you deliberately merge your energy with someone else—such as when you practice exercise 2.6, or after intimate physical contact.

As I'm sure you have noticed, the exercises build upon each other, and will continue to do so. It's a good idea at this point to go back and repeat the ones you may have had trouble with. Remember—the more you practice the skills taught here, the easier later chapters will be for you and, eventually, the more powerful your spells will be. I'm very excited that we've gotten this far, because now we're getting to the fun part.

three

Manipulating Energy

THE ENERGY THAT YOU SEND out into the world, both positive and negative, creates the reality around you. These energies are very powerful and primal; once released, it's almost impossible to call them back, and believe me, you get what you give. Wiccans will be familiar with the Rule of Three: whatever you send out, good or bad, comes back to you at three times the strength of the original energy. If you send out negative or manipulative energy, then that same type of energy will be reflected back to you, threefold. So before we continue, I want you to ask yourself whether you're willing to accept the consequences of your actions. There is no safety net here; you cannot confess your sins and expect the repercussions simply to go away. As we've already discussed, you have to stay "on message." If the message you're sending out is manipulative, hurtful, or destructive, then you should expect results that are manipulative, hurtful, or destructive. It is very important to enter into this covenant with the universe with your eyes wide open—to understand that by taking action, you take on the consequences of your actions, good and bad. If you don't think you can do this, I understand; having power frightens many.

You have the power to change your reality and the world around you, and your primary tool is energy. In the previous chapter, we learned how to sense and connect with this elemental force. In this chapter, we will learn how to *change* energy. Changing, controlling, and directing energy is the very foundation of spellwork. When casting a spell, we use our intent to shape the energy around us, causing it to bend to our will and bring us what we want. Our free will is another powerful tool. We'll learn how to deliberately claim our will and influence the world around us in a way that furthers our individual goals. But at the same time, we need to realize that free will can be dangerous; it needs to be understood and controlled. Spells are the ultimate exercise of free will.

There are many ways of raising energy to power our spells. Perhaps the easiest way is to bring it up from the earth, drawing it up through your chakras using visualization. You can also raise energy through chant, dance, or song; this is especially fun if you do it in a group. Sex is also a good way of becoming energized, but since this book is rated PG-13, you'll have to learn about that on your own. There are other, darker ways of raising energy, but we won't touch those here either.

After we learn how to raise energy, we'll discuss how to direct it. When you direct energy, you are imbuing it with purpose and taking the first step toward setting your spell in motion. You can direct energy in various ways: through touch, visualization, speech, or even thought. This process can be as simple or complex as you'd like, and can also be fun. It is important to try different ways of raising and building energy to find the ones that work best for you. Since spellwork is inherently personal, there is no preset formula that will work for every situation or for every person. Feel free to experiment and develop your own methods.

One of the first things that you need to learn to be able to effectively manipulate energy is how to use emotional cues. Emotional cues are the myriad things that trigger a visceral—instinctive, instantaneous, and powerful—response in us. This part of our brain can react strongly to something as deceptively simple as a color. For example, think about a bullfight; the bulls are trained to react violently to the color red. When they see red, they become enraged and attack. Our unconscious minds react similarly. When an emotion is triggered, we react without effort.

Thus color can be a powerful emotional cue. As we discussed in chapter 2, some people perceive energy as color. But even if you don't perceive energy that way, color is important to our perceptions; we associate colors with emotions and attitudes. Some colors make us feel powerful, while other colors make us feel invisible. Color can change the way we view a person, a place, or a situation. We use color to mark correspondences in Wicca; we also use it in sympathetic magick and in candle magick. In our first exercise, we'll use color as a gateway to unlocking the energy of our emotions.

EXERCISE 3.1

Color as an emotional cue

For this exercise you will need:

> *Ten minutes*
> *A quiet place where you won't be disturbed*

Many magical books include charts and lists of color correspondences. These are interesting to read, if rather arbitrary, but they are of little use for our purposes. Instead, take a few minutes and meditate on what colors you associate with the following emotions. When you are clear about each response, write it down.

Anger _____

Love _____

Sadness _____

Apathy _____

Joy _____

Happiness _____

Sexiness _____

Power _____

Fear _____

Pain _____

Anguish _____

Defeat _____

Peace _____

Frustration _____

Protection _____

Cowardice _____

Serenity _____

Indifference _____

Regret _____

Desire _____

Sincerity _____

Intelligence _____

Protectiveness _____

Loneliness _____

Excitement _____

Prosperity _____

Delight _____

Rejection _____

Righteousness _____

Pride _____

Loveliness _____

Faith _____

Assuredness _____

Detachment _____

Vengefulness _____

Confidence _____

Worry _____

Shyness _____

Illness _____

Timidity _____

Sorrow _____

Hatred _____

Bravery _____

*Nervousness*_____

Cheerfulness _____

Adventurousness _____

There are no right or wrong answers here. What's important is recognizing your own emotional associations and triggers that you have built up over the course of your lifetime. These intuitive associations are already in place within you, and I don't see any need to reinvent the wheel by teaching you an arbitrary set of correspondences that might not work for you. Using your own correspondences is far more effective.

Let me give you an example: I cannot stand the color yellow. It reminds me of piss, of blond girls who picked on me in school, of being angry and not being able to do anything about it. This is the color I associate with anger, but someone else might associate it with happiness. To them, yellow might represent sunny days spent playing in the sand on the beach, or it might be the color of the sundress they wore when they had their first kiss. You get the idea. Thinking of yellow is enough to change my mood; if I want to project a feeling of anger, even when I'm not angry, I focus on the color yellow.

In the next exercise, we'll learn how to raise emotional energy based on our response to a color.

Using color to raise energy

For this exercise you will need:

Twenty to thirty minutes

As always, pick a quiet place where you won't be disturbed, and sit comfortably or lie down. Take a few moments to quiet your thoughts and relax your body. Now think about the colors from the prior exercise, and choose one that corresponds to a positive emotion like love, joy, or peace. When you're ready, close your eyes. In your mind's eye, visualize your chosen color. Surround yourself with it. See its texture, its brightness, its intensity. The color fills your inner landscape. When every part of everything you visualize is filled with this color, hold it there.

As you look within, think of all the reasons you associate the emotion you wrote on your list with the color you chose. Build the reasons within your mind. Let your mind travel to the places where you felt that emotion and saw the color. Let the emotion flood your consciousness, along with the color, until you can no longer distinguish one from the other. As this happens, you notice that the color you've held within your mind's eye is no longer just a color. It swirls and pulsates, moving to the rhythm of your heart. Each heartbeat amplifies the color and makes it stronger, pulls the emotion closer and makes it more intense. As the emotion and energy become even more powerful, your heart beats faster.

When you feel as full of this emotion as possible, notice the energy around you. This is the energy you've raised simply by drawing on a particular emotion. Every time you see this particular color, you will associate it with this feeling. The color will act as a trigger for you, taking you back to this point where the emotion is intense and your energy is high.

Do you notice a difference between the way your personal energy felt in exercise 2.1 and now? Take a moment to focus on the differences. When you fully comprehend the contrast in both intensity and sheer amount of energy, you're ready to move on to the next step.

You noticed that, as the emotion became more intense, your heart rate increased. Now focus on returning it to a more normal rate. Visualize the pulsation and movement of the color slowing as your heartbeat slows; see the color begin to fade from your mind's eye. Starting at the edge of your energy field, drain the excess energy—and the emotion associated with it—into the earth through your root chakra, returning your energy field to its normal color, size, and intensity. Release the color and the emotion, and thank them, knowing you can draw on their power anytime.

Note that this final step, known as grounding, is not necessary if you use this technique in a spell. When you raise energy for a spell, you will release the energy into an object or into the world to manifest your goal. You won't return the energy back to the earth as we did here. Since this exercise has no tangible purpose beyond the experience itself, you must ground the excess energy and emotion so you don't carry it around with you needlessly.

How did you feel after this exercise? Were you more energized or did you need a nap? Some people may feel a little more sensitive or emotional afterward. This will pass, but if you feel a little too intense, gather the excess energy and push it out of your body and energy field and into the earth, just as we did in exercise 2.7. Allow it to drain out until you feel more balanced. This can also help you control emotional excesses in other situations.

Exercises 3.3, 3.4, and 3.5 will introduce more active methods of raising energy. We'll begin with chant, which can be a very powerful way of raising energy since it helps focus the mind on a single issue. You can use any single word or series of words to create a chant. Rhythmic sound becomes the medium for the energy; you will use the volume of your voice, the beat of the drum, or your clapping to control the intensity of the energy raised. When working in a group, chant has the positive side effect of helping to attain group mind; also, each member of the group can chant a different word to create a counterpoint of energy.

Dance as a tool operates similarly, but adds the element of physical activity to rhythm. You may be surprised to learn that movement can be fun as well as powerful. Think of Native Americans or tribal Africans dancing around ritual fires. There is so much energy and power in just watching them. How much more dynamic do you think it would be to do the dancing yourself? I love to dance; I look for any excuse to move around, shake my hips, and have some fun. Don't worry about looking silly. You don't have to be a professional, and you don't even have to be particularly good—you just have to have fun and enjoy the experience. Even if you're working in a group, everyone will be too focused on their own feet to notice yours. If you are working alone, well then, it's just you and the rhythm.

Song differs from chant in several important ways. Chant is simple; it has a rhythm but no melody. Song is more complex; you vary the sounds, change the pitch, use more words. Anything can be turned into a song. If you are struggling for ideas, try using "do re mi fa so la ti do." Just as with the dance exercise, you don't have to be a professional or sing like Pavarotti or Ella Fitzgerald. The important thing here is to really put your heart and soul into it. If you wonder whether song can be powerful, think about the "high" musicians are known to feel at the end of a concert, or the emotion and energy you've felt when you've attended a concert. This is the power of song.

Combining song or chant with dance is a variation you can experiment with on your own. As an example, think about the energy of the choir in a charismatic church, how they sing and move and get the entire congregation involved. They are able to raise a great deal of strong energy. Think how powerful that would be directed into spellwork!

As you work your way through the exercises, it's a good idea to wait a couple hours between each one. If you are very inexperienced, you may want to wait a day or two between exercises.

EXERCISE 3.3

Using chant to raise energy

For this exercise you will need:

> *Ten to fifteen minutes*
> *A small drum (if you don't have one, you can clap your hands)*

This is probably my favorite way to raise energy. It is fun, simple, and very intense; it is also one of the easiest methods to control and direct. The word or words you chant should be directly related to the intent of your spell; for example, if doing a money spell, you can simply repeat the word "money" over and over.

Sit comfortably with your drum and take a moment to get centered. Say "mo-ney" aloud, slowly, and strike the drum as you speak each syllable. Gradually increase your speed until the word gets one drumbeat rather than two: "money, money, money."

You will notice something interesting as you continue: the chant seems to take on a life of its own. The words come faster and are spoken more loudly, the beat increases. Go on until you are sure you understand how raising this energy feels.

When you are doing spellwork, you will release the energy at the most intense point (the crescendo). But for the purpose of this exercise, when you reach the crescendo and can't possibly increase the intensity any further, force yourself to pull back and begin slowing down the chant. Go gradually from a swift drumbeat and a loud, almost shouted "money" to a slower rhythm and a softer voice. The last "money" will be almost whispered and will once again be accompanied by two drumbeats: "mo-ney."

How did this feel? Were you more energized or did you feel a little tired? What did you notice, if anything, at the point when you stopped chanting? I usually notice an almost audible "pop" as the energy releases.

If you're not used to working with large amounts of energy or you feel too energized, you may want to take a moment and release the excess into the earth. You can do this passively, simply by making contact with the ground, or by using the technique learned in exercise 2.7. Release just enough energy to return you to your normal energy level. Holding onto too much energy can give you a headache or make you restless or anxious.

Using dance to raise energy

For this exercise you will need:

> *Fifteen to twenty minutes*
> *A recording of a favorite song with a strong beat that starts slowly and builds over time*
> *An open area where you won't fall or trip on anything*
> *Optional: a small drum that you can easily carry as you dance*

Put on the song, pick up your drum if you're using one, and start moving. Begin slowly and move with simple, easy motions. Your dance doesn't need to follow any particular steps; just follow the music. As the beat increases, pick up your pace. If you are drumming, increase the speed and intensity of the drumbeat. Keep going, picking up the pace and moving faster and faster.

Just as with the chanting in the previous exercise, you should notice your dancing taking on a life of its own, growing in intensity and speed. I often feel as if I'm a child again, whirling around in a circle. If you are dancing to raise energy for a spell, you will want to stop at the crescendo and release the energy. But for the exercise, gradually begin slowing down your motions and your drumming, bringing yourself down until you are once more moving with slow, easy motions, and then stop. Take a moment to ground if you feel the need.

How did this feel? Was it fun? I always feel like collapsing on the couch after raising energy this way, but I almost always have a big grin on my face as I lie there. This method puts you in touch with your inner child and reconnects you with the silliness of life. It's a good reminder that spellwork doesn't have to be solemn and serious—it should be fun.

EXERCISE 3.5

Using song to raise energy

For this exercise you will need:

> *Fifteen to twenty minutes*
> *A recording of a favorite song with a strong beat that starts slowly and builds over time*
> *Optional: a small drum (if you don't have one, you can clap your hands)*

This exercise is very similar to the previous two. Begin singing along with your recording, softly and slowly, and follow the rhythm as it gradually builds to the crescendo. If using this method in spellwork, you'll want to release the energy at the highest point, but for this exercise, gradually reduce your speed and intensity until you are once again singing softly and slowly. You can also sing a song from memory, without using a recording. If utilizing song in conjunction with spellwork, always choose one with lyrics that are "on message" to create your desired result.

How did this exercise feel? Were you able to let go and enjoy the experience?

EXERCISE 3.6

Raising energy from the earth

For this exercise you will need:

> *Fifteen to twenty minutes*
> *A quiet place where you won't be disturbed*

This exercise builds upon what we learned in exercise 2.4. Take a moment to re-read it before starting. When you are ready, sit comfortably with your back straight, close your eyes, and make sure your mind is centered and your body is relaxed. Follow the steps of exercise 2.4 to the point when your energy tendrils have merged with the energy of the earth. This time, instead of just sensing the earth's energy, you will begin pulling it up through your tendrils to the base of your spine and your root chakra. Feel it flow from the earth into your root chakra, and feel it spread upward through each of your major chakras. Then focus on drawing the earth energy down your arms to the two lesser chakras in your palms. Take a moment to get used to how that feels.

Turn your dominant hand so that it is palm up, and focus on the energy that is centered there. Push the energy out through the open chakra in the palm of your hand so that it forms a little energy ball. Let this energy ball rest in the palm of your hand. Open your eyes; can you see the energy ball? What does it look like? Now hold your receiving hand over your dominant hand. Let it rest just above the energy ball. Can you feel it? What does it feel like?

With energy from your dominant hand, push up the energy ball until it is touching the open chakra in your receiving hand. Focus on the energy center in your receiving hand and direct it to take in the energy ball. Feel the chakra absorb the ball until it melds completely with the rest of the energy there. How did that feel? Now reverse the process, and use your receiving hand to return the energy ball to your dominant hand. Feel free to play with the ball of energy, learning how it responds to your intent.

When you are ready, ground the excess energy by returning it to the earth through your tendrils, then withdraw your tendrils from the earth as you did in exercise

2.4. After you're done, you may want to ground yourself again; this experience is usually pretty intense.

In spellwork, you can use the energy ball you created to direct earth energy into an inanimate object like a candle, or you can imbue the energy ball with intent and release it. If you are working with other individuals, you can take an energy ball from another person through your receiving hand, add some of your own energy to it, and pass it on to the next participant. You can continue this cycle until the group has a large ball of energy, which can be directed into an object or released into the world. The possible applications of this type of energy work are almost endless.

Was there one way of raising energy that worked best for you, or one that you liked better than the others? Which was it, and why? Was there a method that didn't work as well for you? Did you attempt to combine methods? If so, were the results better or worse than using just one technique? Most of the time, in solitary spellwork or when working with others, I use a combination of the techniques in exercises 3.3 to 3.5.

The more you work with these methods, the more intense the experience will become, and the more energy you'll be able to draw and channel at one time. I strongly recommend that you commit thirty days to energy work. Pick one or more of the energy-raising methods from this chapter and work with it once a day. In a small journal or in your Book of Shadows, record your experiences. It's important to note your results, because when we move on to spellwork, you'll want to utilize the most effective method(s) possible to raise energy to power your spells. When I did this, I noticed that after thirty days of practice, I could raise the energy to the same level as I had on the prior day, on command. So every time I did the exercise, the energy I raised was exponentially greater than the day before.

What you are actually doing is conditioning yourself to raise energy and, by extension, training your mind to expect a particular result. I'm sure you've heard about Russian scientist Ivan Pavlov's experiments with his dogs. Every time he fed the dogs, he rang a bell. The dogs would salivate when they saw the food. After a while, Pavlov didn't bring the food, but he rang the bell, and he noticed that the dogs still salivated. They were conditioned or trained to salivate each time they heard the bell in expectation of food. This is known as a *conditioned reflex.* You can do the same thing with your mind: you begin to chant and your mind provides the energy because that is what it expects to happen.

When I found Wicca after moving to the U.S., I became distracted by complex, ritualized spellwork (this is common among new witches). Just as with Pavlov and his dogs, using complex techniques can create conditioning that builds an association between ritual steps and power; the more you repeat a ritual over and over, the more powerful it becomes. Take, for example, a Catholic mass. If you have never seen one, I recommend waking up early one Sunday and watching one on television. There is so much history and ritual in each element of the mass that even a viewer at home can feel its power.

Energy work and spellwork can be as simple or as complex as you desire. I always try to keep things simple. Simple saves time, effort, and expense, and can be just as powerful as a more complicated working. I also like simple because that was what my Jeda did best. She did her healing with little fanfare, making use of everyday things. But even though her workings were simple, they were highly effective, often bringing better results than more complicated solutions suggested by others.

Now that we've learned a few ways to raise energy, it's time to learn how to manipulate it. This means modifying the energy and imbuing it with intent. Energy itself is neither good nor bad; it doesn't carry intent. It's up to the witch to add intent to the energy—in other words, to program it to accomplish the witch's goal—and then to direct the energy, which sends it into the world or into an object.

In the next exercise, you will raise energy charged with intent, "store" it in a cauldron while you build the energy to the crescendo, and then release the energy to do your will. Most Wiccans will have a cauldron dedicated solely to spellwork; if you don't, use a clean cooking pot or a large, sturdy metal mixing bowl.

EXERCISE 3.7

Directing energy

For this exercise you will need:

> *Ten to fifteen minutes*
> *A cauldron or other metal container*

Choose a method from exercises 3.3, 3.4, or 3.5 to raise energy. Begin as directed in the exercise, focusing on your intent—for example, drawing money to you. Then, as the chant/dance/song builds in intensity, visualize a mini-cyclone of pure energy building around you. Imbue this energy with your intent; if you are chanting "money," visualize the energy taking on the characteristics and colors you associate with money—think of the color of sparkling gold coins, or the scent and texture of a crisp, brand-new hundred dollar bill. Now visualize this powerful force moving at your command, spiraling into the cauldron as you continue to chant/dance/sing. When you reach the crescendo and can't possibly build more intensity, instead of slowing down and taking the energy back as in the initial exercise, direct the energy to explode out of the cauldron. See it and feel it rushing out into the world to bring you what you want. You will probably want to ground yourself afterward.

Here is a variation using the technique from exercise 3.6. Follow the directions until you once again have the energy ball sitting in the palm of your dominant hand. But this time, feed it energy until it is about the size of a basketball, and visualize it taking on the intent of your working. If you are doing a love spell, see it turning the color you associate with love (pink, for example) and saturate it as thoroughly as possible with your intent (to bring you a compatible lover, for example). Throw the energy ball into the air and direct it to explode as it goes up, like fireworks. See it and feel it showering energy around you as it heads out into the world to bring you what you want. Return any excess energy to the earth.

Now that we've discussed the necessary building blocks, we're ready to move on to charging objects for a specific purpose. Charging an object is actually quite simple and employs techniques you've already learned. After raising energy and imbuing it with your intent, you will direct it into an object for a specific purpose. Unlike the previous exercise, there is no energy release at the end; instead, the object becomes a container of energy charged with intent, and it will retain that energy until directed to release it.

Candles are among the most common objects that witches charge. Generally they are used, and used up, in a spell; they don't remain as a tangible, continuous piece of magick on their own. You infuse the candle with energy and intent, which are released when the candle is consumed by fire, and the energy goes out into the world to accomplish the task it is charged with. Other objects, such as charms, are also infused with energy and intent, but unlike candles, they are not used up during spellwork and remain as a tangible piece of magick.

There are two basic types of charms. The first type is simply meant to be a visual cue that reminds the witch of a working and reinforces her mindset to stay "on message." It's the easiest type of charm to create and a central part of folk magic. These charms do not contain any sort of charged energy, but they act to reinforce intent. This was the kind my great-grandmother used most often. For example, she would give a sprig of dried jasmine to a girl seeking a husband and ask her to keep it on her at all times. She would also counsel the girl on how to go about finding a husband, such as wearing red to attract attention, and going out more often, particularly to weddings, where the guests are already thinking about marriage. The jasmine itself was just a dried flower, but to the girl it represented reaching her goal. Every time she saw it, she remembered the advice Jeda gave her, and it had the added effect of giving her extra confidence.

The second type of charm is more complex. Its primary goal is to hold energy charged with intent for spellworking. While these charms sometimes do double duty, working in the same way as the first type we discussed, that isn't their primary intent. In order to create this type of charm, we first need to learn how to charge objects.

EXERCISE 3.8

Charging objects

For this exercise you will need:
> *Fifteen to twenty minutes*
> *Three or four inanimate objects*

As always, choose an appropriate place where you won't be disturbed. Sit comfortably and take a moment to get centered. Hold one of the objects in your receiving hand. Using the technique from exercise 3.6, create an energy ball in the palm of your dominant hand. Focus your attention on the energy ball and charge it with your intent. For example, if you're doing a love spell, you would project feelings of love, completeness, and contentedness that you feel when you are with your lover. As you do this, visualize the energy ball taking on the color you associate with love, such as a nice bright pink. When the energy ball is as full of your intent as you can manage, hold your dominant hand over the object in your receiving hand and direct the energy to flow into the object. Visualize a stream of energy flooding into and around the object, suffusing it completely with your intent.

When you are done, put the object down and pick up the next one. Draw up more energy from the earth if you need to, then repeat the above procedure. Make it a point to charge each object with a different intent. If you are working with a living or once-living thing, you will want to ask it for assistance. For example, figs represent abundance, so if I am doing a money spell I might use a fig as a representative. Before I do anything, I will ask it for permission, and for its help in transforming the energy I'm directing. Remember, everything around us has its own energy. Working against the energy already inherent in an object is counterproductive; it's easier just to add energy than to replace it.

When you have worked your way through all the objects you selected, return any excess energy to the earth. You might also want to rub or clap your hands together lightly to clear the palm chakras.

Each object will feel different once it is charged. Allow an hour or two to pass, then go back to your charged objects. Pick one up. How does it feel compared to a similar but uncharged object? How does the object you charged with love (for example) feel different from one charged with a differing intent?

Charging a candle

Not all charged objects are charms, but all charms are charged objects. Let me give you an example of a useful, everyday charm. I have a purple sarong that I bought at a Renaissance faire when I was eighteen. It has traveled with me on many journeys. I've used it as a blanket, a pillow, a dress, a skirt, a sofa cover, and a curtain, and it's currently hanging from hooks on a wall in my bedroom like a tapestry. Even though this sarong has many mundane uses, its primary use is as a protection charm. When I bought it, I charged it with protection. I reinforce its charge each year at Samhain (Halloween). Having the sarong with me makes me feel protected—not because the sarong itself has any magical properties, but because I know it holds protective energy that will act when necessary to keep me safe.

You've probably noticed by now that our "exercises" are gradually turning into spells. In the next exercise, you will create a usable charm for whatever purpose you choose.

Charging objects is an important skill to master. Objects can be charged in two ways: they can be directed to carry energy, or they can be imbued with a particular emotion.

To charge an object with a particular emotion, follow these steps:

Step one: Select the object and emotion you would like to charge. For this exercise, I recommend using a candle. If you use a candle, refer to the color association created in exercise 3.1 when selecting your candle. If you cannot find a candle of the color you need, use a white candle for any positive emotion or a black candle for negative emotions. Then, as you work on the candle, focus on turning the candle in your mind's eye into one of the color you associate with the particular emotion.

Step two: Hold the candle firmly in one hand. Draw up energy from the earth, and, as you bring it up, feel it settle into your core.

Step three: Once you have a good amount of energy drawn, direct it down your empty hand until it settles into a ball at the palm of your hand. Focus on the emotional triggers from the beginning of the chapter, the texture of the energy, the color you associate with the emotion. Direct the energy ball, focusing it until it takes on the characteristics and the feeling of the emotion you want to direct into the candle. (The stronger the emotion is within you, the easier it will be to direct the energy to take on the emotion you desire. For the first attempt at this, I recommend working with a positive emotion that you are familiar with.)

Step four: Once the energy has taken on the required characteristics, move the hand with the energy ball until it is hovering above the hand with the candle, palm up. Slowly turn your hand over until the energy ball is directly over the candle. Then lower your hand, directing the energy so that it is absorbed by the candle.

Step five: Clear any residual energy retained by returning the energy to the earth as directed in prior exercises.

This type of exercise is very good for getting rid of excess or unwanted emotions. Burn the candle after charging it to release the energy. This exercise is also good for a different purpose—if you are confronted by a person you would like to get rid of, charge a small gift, directing the energy to take on the desire you have to make the person do what you want. Then, once the gift is charged, give it to the person and watch what happens.

Note: This last part is slightly manipulative, and you should weigh the moral and ethical considerations associated with such a working.

To charge a candle with energy, simply omit steps three and four.

EXERCISE 3.10

Creating a charm

For this exercise you will need:

> *Twenty minutes*
> *Two candles charged with intent that corresponds to the charm you plan to create*
> *An object to be used permanently as a charm*

Ideally, the object you select for this exercise should mean something to you, and be of a size you can easily keep with you. For example, if you want to attract love, you might use a small rose quartz heart. If you want to attract money, you might use a foreign coin or a faux gold piece (it's best not to use common pocket change; you don't want to accidentally spend your charm!).

Choose an appropriate location where you won't be disturbed and seat yourself comfortably. Take a moment to get centered. Using one of the energy-raising techniques discussed earlier in the chapter, charge the object just as you did in exercise 3.8 (I suggest using the same method of energy raising you used to charge the candles in exercise 3.9). Visualize the object becoming a container that can hold and redirect the energy you will give it. Since names have power, you will also want to name the object according to its purpose. For example, if you're using a rose quartz heart to attract a partner, you could name it Romantic Love. If you're chanting to raise power, chant the name of the object while visualizing it becoming the container. When you're ready, send the energy you've raised into your object.

Next, place the candles on either side of the charged object, and light them (working on a fireproof surface, of course). Visualize the energy you placed into the candles being released. See it form a sphere of energy, imbued with your intent, which hovers above and around your object. Now visualize that energy flowing into the object, much like pouring water into a glass, completely suffusing the object with power. Meditate on that image until you feel done. Allow the candles to burn down, releasing all their energy into the charm, then dispose of the candle remnants.

Your charm is now ready to use. Not only will it serve as a tangible reminder of your intent, it will also continually act as a "battery," releasing its stored energy to manifest your desire.

Thus far, all the exercises in this chapter have been about raising and directing energy on your own. However, it's likely that you won't always work alone. Learning to work in a group setting when you are used to solitary work can be a challenge, particularly if you are working with other solitaries who also have limited group experience.

Group work can be fun and very powerful, or it can be stressful and a failure. Its outcome greatly depends on the level of trust between the participants, among other factors. In general, people who have known each other for a while and who have good rapport are most likely to have a successful working. The success or failure of a group working is dependent on five things:

1. The skill/experience of the group members
2. The commitment each member brings to the working
3. The level of trust/familiarity among members
4. The design of the working itself
5. The skill of the priest/priestess in achieving group mind and directing the energy

If all the above elements are positive, then the likelihood of success is very high, but if even one element is lacking, the working will probably fail. Think about your own experiences if you have worked with a group in the past. What was your most successful spell? What was your most dismal failure? Which spells had mixed outcomes? Most importantly, why do you think they worked or didn't work?

In group work, you won't always be the one in charge. Sometimes you will have to be a follower, and other times you will have to step up to the plate and lead.

As a follower, your job is to:

- Channel your energy to the leader
- Follow his or her directions
- Have fun and enjoy the experience

As a leader, your job is to:

- Direct the energy of the other group members
- Provide directions that facilitate achieving group mind
- Make sure that everyone is enjoying the experience (including yourself)

It's important to be able to do a good job as both leader and follower. Some people are uncomfortable stepping up and taking control, while others can't stand to take directions from someone else. My solution is to take baby steps: put yourself in positions that challenge your comfort levels a little at a time.

The next exercise provides an introduction to energy work with a group. It can be done with as few as two people, but three or more would be ideal.

Energy work with others

For this exercise you will need:

> *Thirty minutes*
> *One or more partners*
> *A cauldron*

I'd like you to perform this group exercise twice, so that you can try on the roles of both leader and follower. It's best to let a minimum of twenty-four hours pass between attempts.

Discuss with your partner(s) which of the energy-raising methods from this chapter you will use and who will be leader first. Next, decide what intent you would like to channel, what word or words you will use if chanting, and what word or words you will use to release the energy at the end.

As the leader, you will be in control of the drum, clapping, or song. Controlling the tempo and raising the energy level will be up to you. As a follower, you will need to listen for the changes in tempo and volume; as the leader starts chanting louder and faster, you chant louder and faster. As the leader, you can't get lost in the energy; you have to pay close attention to the pace and decide when you are approaching the crescendo. As a follower, you have more freedom to get lost, as you can trust the leader to direct you at the right time.

We will be using the technique from exercise 3.7, so go back and re-read it. But for the purposes of this exercise, the followers will send their energy to the leader, and the leader will send it into the cauldron. When the energy has reached the crescendo, the leader will indicate when it's time to release it, and everyone may want to shout something related to the intent of the spell, for example, "Bring us a good harvest!" This will trigger the energy release. Whether acting as leader or follower, make sure that you visualize the energy exploding from the cauldron and going out into the world.

What was your experience with the exercise as leader? As a follower? Do you prefer one role or the other?

When working with a group or another witch, it's important that you understand the situation you're stepping into and the motives that drive your companions. If you don't and you act anyway, you will pay any consequences alongside your friends—regardless of how noble your intentions might be. The first time I worked with another witch to cast a spell, I was nineteen. I'd just finished my first year of college and was home for the summer. A good friend from high school needed help getting out of a bad situation. At the same time, she also wanted a little revenge for the wrongs done to her. Unfortunately, revenge disguised as justice can backfire in many ways, particularly if you bear any of the fault for the situation. I'd been away at college that whole year and hadn't been around to witness the mutually self-destructive behavior practiced by both my friend and her "abusive" boyfriend.

Since anger and jealousy are powerful emotions, they are excellent fuel for spells. The energy created from those emotions would be enough for a nuclear meltdown, and that was the energy I decided we would redirect to bring "justice" to the situation. My friend, thinking that justice in this case would be a one-way street, enthusiastically agreed to put "the whammy," as she called it, on her ex.

I found a likely spell in one of the books I owned. We got together one evening to modify it and I made two copies. We decided that the spell should be cast on the full moon, four days away, when drawing energy would be at its strongest. However, over the intervening days I felt uneasy about casting the spell. I put my feelings down to not having done group spellwork before, and to being unused to working with the particular goddess we were calling on for help.

It's important to realize that justice is never a one-way street, and that the universe will hold everyone involved equally accountable for his or her role in the matter. Furthermore, if you ask for justice from Kali, the Hindu goddess of destruction, and you bear at least 50 percent of the blame for the situation, you'd better expect to pay 50 percent or more of the cost. This force, once unleashed, will turn on the witch if he or she is in any way responsible for what happened. There will also be consequences for anyone else involved in the spellcasting, regardless of how innocent of the situation they are. I warned my friend that Kali wasn't the kind of goddess to call on if you were guilty yourself and seeking "justice." But she insisted that she bore no blame for the situation. Since she was one of my closest friends and I was inclined to trust her, I said okay.

We cast the spell at moonrise on the night of the full moon, and things started happening the next day. My friend's ex was picked up by the police when they found drugs in the car he was driving after he was stopped for running a red light. Unfortunately, it was her car and it was impounded. The apartment they'd shared was still listed as his address (even though she'd kicked him out), so the following day the police came with a warrant and tore up the place, looking for more drugs. (Thankfully, they didn't find anything.) So her ex went to jail, but my friend had to pay the impound fees for the car and deal with the destruction of her home by the police. For my part, I lost a good friend because she blamed me for the spell backfiring, even though I'd warned her.

The lesson I learned from this is simple—don't cast spells with someone else unless:

1. They know what they're doing
2. You understand the *entire* situation, not just what your friend told you
3. You are familiar enough with the energies you are calling on, particularly divine energies, to understand how severe the consequences might be
4. You are willing to pay the price if things don't work out as planned

In the next chapter, we'll move on to actual spellcasting. Chapter four will focus on how to take a spell from a book or the Internet and make it your own. Although most experienced witches write their own spells (which we'll explore later in the chapter), there is something to be said for taking the occasional shortcut. Just as in group work, make sure you understand what you are doing and the energies you are tapping into when you use a spell written by another person. If you don't feel comfortable working with a particular energy or deity, don't do it. It's important to trust your instincts more than you trust the author of a spell or a book (even me!).

four

Revising Existing Spells
and
Writing Your Own

WALK INTO ANY NEW AGE store, or into the New Age section of the major chain bookstores, and you can find them—spell books! They range from the serious to the silly. Many of them are designed with zany fonts, bright colors, or lovely illustrations to make them instantly appealing. I've even seen spell cards and spell-a-day calendars. Some of my more serious "witchy" friends look at these books, roll their eyes, and say "Ugh!"

Not me—I love them. To me, spell books mean that I don't have to sit down and think of words that rhyme. They give me new ideas for spellcasting and—let's be honest—they can be fun. For example, I never would have thought to use a bubble bath for spellwork until I read about it. Fancy spell books cater to the self-indulgent part of us, the part that eats expensive chocolates, watches *Sex and the City,* and splurges occasionally on an expensive dress or shoes.

I know what you're thinking: spells from those books don't work. That may be true, but there's an easy fix. For the most part, those spells are missing a crucial ingredient:

energy—and you've just learned how to raise and direct energy quite effectively. I know that I'm going to get criticized by some witches who think that the only way to cast a spell is to write your own from scratch. But in this busy day and age, we don't have time to make everything from scratch—we buy bread at the supermarket, we bake our cakes from a mix, even our dinners come from a box. We take shortcuts where we can; why should spellwork be any different?

I want you to think of that type of spell book as a sort of magical cake mix. You get all the dry ingredients and you just have to add water or an egg—or, in this case, energy. The only time you run into a problem is when you think of "instant" spells as being complete as written; after all, cake mix doesn't taste good if you eat it from the box! But add some time and the necessary ingredients and you've made a lovely and tasty treat.

I'm not telling you to go out to Barnes & Noble and buy thirty of these books. But if you already have some or if you see one that appeals to you by all means get it. I bought one unknowingly when I was a teen, and I got one as a gift from a friend who was not Wiccan but who was trying to be open minded. Since then I've picked up some of the books knowing exactly what they are on my own. I don't believe in wasting any resources, so I've worked through quite a few of the spells in those books in the past few years and tailored them to work for me. I also don't believe in doing more work than is absolutely necessary, so if I can find someone who already took the time to think out an entire spell that works for me with little changes, why not use it?

Of course, some of the spells in books are really quite absurd, unrealistic, or just plain silly. That doesn't mean that magick doesn't work for the absurd, unrealistic, or silly. If you think about it, most people don't believe in magick. They look down on witches for being kooky or just plain crazy. If they love you or are related, then you're eccentric. But if they are particularly intolerant, they might call for the guys in the white coats or perhaps an exorcist.

As witches, we need to learn to take things lightly and enjoy the absurd. Those of us who can't laugh at ourselves (and at those who think us insane!) will eventually become negative and bitter. I'm not saying you shouldn't take your spellwork seriously, but joking around and laughing raises positive energy that can also be directed toward the goal of the spell. Laughing makes you feel good—it releases chemicals that make your brain happy, and by extension the rest of you feels good.

A positive attitude was the cornerstone of Jeda's spellwork. She would sing love songs to the herbs in her garden. When women came to her, seeking love or troubled by marital problems, she never made them feel bad. She didn't create elaborate ceremonies, light thirty candles, or go skyclad at midnight on the night of the full moon. She would have laughed if anyone had suggested she do that. Instead, she gently made suggestions or mixed tinctures and tonics, and generally her cures were simple. I remember one occasion when a girl and her mother came to ask Jeda to help the girl find a husband. After talking with them for about thirty minutes, Jeda went into the kitchen and came back with a bunch of fresh mint. She gave it to them with instructions that the girl should chew on a sprig every time she went out. Doing this, Jeda said, would help her find a husband before the year was out. After they left, I asked Jeda why she had given the women mint, since she usually gave women seeking love jasmine flowers and told them to put some under their beds and in their bras. Jeda laughed and said, "Didn't you smell her breath?"

Remembering this story always makes me laugh, and it reminds me that all that's necessary to fix many of our problems is something simple, like a sprig of mint and fresh breath. Having the mint gave the girl confidence that she had help in reaching her goal, and it had the secondary effect of giving her minty fresh breath. This is the essence of magick—it provides a little "push" to give us some help in meeting a need on our own.

A good spell has three parts:

1. A clearly stated goal
2. A sympathetic link between the mundane and magical

3. A way of raising energy that links the mundane and magical |

In general, most spells have the first two in abundance. They have a goal such as finding true love. They ask you to gather things like two red candles, a piece of paper, and a bottle of perfume, which are intended to link the physical world symbolically with your goal (red candles for passion, perfume for attraction). This is the most basic form of sympathetic magick, the idea that similar things have similar energy and share a connection.

Then these spells ask you to perform actions like lighting the two candles, writing the name of your true love on the piece of paper, anointing the paper with the perfume, and finally, burning the paper by setting it on fire with the flame of the candles. As the paper burns, you're to recite something like, "Smell will bring you to me. When you smell this scent, I will be irresistible to you. So mote it be." Then, the next time you wear that perfume around your true love, he will be irresistibly attracted to you. Simple enough, right?

Can you identify what was missing here? Of course you can: *energy*. Where would you put the energy-raising part of the spell? Let's explore this idea in the next exercise as we modify an existing spell.

Rewriting the "notice me" spell

For this exercise you will need:

Fifteen to twenty minutes

I took this spell from an old Book of Shadows I had in high school. Read through the spell and, in the space provided, note what you would add, subtract, or change. Keep in mind that a little attention can be a good thing, but more is not always better!

Notice me spell

Items needed:

One yellow candle
Parchment paper
Black pen

Steps

On the paper write in black ink:

"I want to see and be seen
I want everyone to know my name
Bring me attention, let me be noticed."

Light the candle while saying the spell.

Burn the paper, and as it burns say, "Notice me!"

Now let's see how your rewrite compares to mine:

Original:

Notice me spell

> Change yellow candle to purple, as I associate purple with positive attention and yellow with anger.

Items needed:

> *One yellow candle*
> *Parchment paper* ←
> *Black pen*

> Use regular unlined paper. No need for expensive parchment paper.
>
> Expense ≠ Results

Steps

On the paper write in black ink:

> *"I want to see and be seen*
> *I want everyone to know my nam*
> *Bring me attention, let me be not*

> Make wording much more specific. Magick takes the path of least resistance, and this version could have dire consequences—meaning the attention it brings could be negative.

Light the candle while saying the spell.

Burn the paper, and as it burns say, "Notice me!"

> These instructions need to be more specific. For example:
>
> Charge the candle as you learned in exercise 3.9, chanting "notice me" while doing so.
> Continue to chant "notice me" as the paper burns.

It's important to remember that magick takes the path of least resistance. Sending out a vague intent like "notice me," without specifying *how* you want to be noticed, is like painting a target on your back. You're asking for something unintended to happen. Instead, your statement of intent needs to be both clear and precise. For example, you could say, "I want my boss [insert his or her name] to notice all the hard work I've been doing and give me a pay raise." This does not give magick a lot of wiggle room; it is short, specific, and hard to misinterpret. I don't mean to imply that the universe is out to get you, but it *will* find the easiest way to give you what you ask for. If it's easier to make a cop notice you speeding than it is to have your boss notice your work, that's what you'll get if you leave it up to the universe.

Let's try a more complicated one:

Rewriting a money spell

For this exercise you will need:

Ten to fifteen minutes

Money spell

Items needed:

3 green candles

Steps

Charge the three candles.

As you light them, say:

"Green as money burn
Bring me what I need
Funds to ease my way
So mote it be."

Let's see how your rewrite compares to mine:

Original version:

Money spell

Items needed:

 3 green candles

Steps

Charge the three candles.

 As you light them, say:

  "Green as money burn

  Bring me what I need

  Funds to ease my way

  So mote it be."

> Using three candles is a bit of overkill. I would change it to one; after all, the candles are each doing the same thing. If I wanted three different things, then I might use three candles, but each one needs to fulfill a specific need.

> Here you're told to charge the candles, but it doesn't say how or with what intent—you are left to guess.

> Just as in the last spell, the intent isn't specific enough. Asking for money without specifying a dollar amount or a particular need is too vague. You could end up finding a penny on the floor!

Putting it all together

Once you have learned the basics of writing a spell and raising energy, it is time to put together all the skills you have learned. One of the essential elements of successful spellwork is timing. It is essential to know when you have gotten to the point where you need to raise energy, how much energy is needed, and when to release the energy at the end of the working. Most of these timing issues are resolved through practice. When working with a spell, it is important to allow an element of spontaneity to enter into the working. Trying to plan all possible aspects and steps of the spell is a good idea, but it is seldom practical, particularly if you are working within a group. Most of the time, the modifications are unintended—a person shows up with the wrong color candle, or something breaks, or you start the spell and cannot remember the words, or you planned the working for six p.m. and you had to stay at work an extra hour and have to start later than expected. Anything can happen. The more rigid you are in your expectations, the more pressure you will place on yourself, and this will hinder the success of the working if the slightest thing goes wrong and you focus on it. One of my teachers calls it the Loki effect. Deal with it or it will deal with you.

Knowing where and when to begin adding the energy to the spell is something you will have to practice. Each spell is different, and what will work perfectly in one spell will not work in another. Much like love, energy can come from unexpected places, and at the least likely time.

Consider what type of energy-raising technique you want to use when you plan the spell. Then think of where the best point to begin adding the energy might be. Once you begin the spell, try to stick to the plan. Make sure you have a written copy of the steps you want to take, the words you plan to say, and the intent of the working. Raise the energy as you planned to, and push the level of energy as high as you possibly can—the more energy the bigger the impact of the spell. Make sure that you are not using your *own* energy reserves; at the end of the spell you should feel alive and energized, like you had a full night of restful sleep. If you feel drained and tired at the end of the working, go back over what you did. Where did you draw the energy from? In most cases the energy should come directly from the earth or a charged object. There are a variety of energy-raising techniques discussed here, and any one or a combination of them can work very well in almost any spell. Consider, though, the rest of the spell before choosing your energy-raising technique. For example, if the spell calls for you sit and meditate, then dancing might not be an appropriate energy-raising method for that type of working.

You can easily revise existing spells to make them more effective and to conform more closely to your needs. Just remember to follow the principles mentioned at the beginning of the chapter. If the language of the spell is too vague, make it more specific; ask for what you want, be blunt, and don't beat around the bush. Asking for "prosperity" is a waste of time when what you really want is a hundred dollars. "Prosperity" can mean a million different things, many of which have nothing to do with money. Asking for "love" is similarly vague. If what you want is a boyfriend, ask for that; otherwise you might end up with a friend you love, new shoes you love, and the love of your parents—but still no boyfriend. Magick is literal; it does not like euphemisms. This is one reason why witches need to be very careful with what they say and do. Magick will take you at your word. If you tell someone to "drop dead," and you put energy and intent into that statement, they might just drop dead, even though what you really meant was "go away."

Know exactly what you want, have a plan in mind for how you want to get it, and guide the spell in that direction. If it is unclear or non-specific, then you can't get angry when you don't get what you expected. At the same time, you want to leave magick a little wiggle room, because it might see something that you didn't. Finding a balance between the two extremes takes practice.

As a witch, you need to be able to write your own spells in addition to using or modifying the work of other people.

Books and spells written by others can only take you so far. At some point you'll have a need that isn't addressed in your books or online. But most importantly, writing your own spell is more personal, which means more of your own energy is invested in it, right from the start.

When I first started trying to write my own spells, my biggest problem was deciding whose theories to follow. Every author has his or her own ideas about how spells should be written, what elements should be included, and even when spells should be performed. As you should realize by now, I prefer the common sense approach, as did my Jeda. The basic premise behind any magical work is intent; I believe that everything else is just pretty window-dressing. Ideally, a witch should be able to cast a complete working spell without the use of a single tool. Unfortunately, this isn't always the case. Since magick works in the subconscious, many people need various trappings or embellishments to access this part of their mind. Traditional ritual magick, for example, requires a great deal of preparation and fanfare. Spells are written and memorized in advance, tools are purchased or made and consecrated, special robes are worn. All these things serve one purpose: they are designed to put the spellcaster in the proper frame of mind for making magick. But are they necessary? In my opinion, no.

You will find that authors of spell books rarely agree about the timing of spellwork, in particular. Some will tell you to perform spells only at night; others will say to do banishing spells at night and drawing spells during the day. Some claim that no spellwork should be done during the new moon, others that only banishing spells should be done then. The more you read, the more contradictory and confusing the theories become. I feel that all these rules are arbitrary and unnecessary. They set up an expectation of failure if everything isn't done just so. Some of the best and most powerful spells I've cast have been spontaneous, performed using the objects at hand and with very little prior preparation.

In my personal spellwork, the phases of the moon are the only correspondences I try to account for (more on that shortly). There are other books that go into a huge amount of detail about the timing of spells and every possible astrological and seasonal correspondence. They'll tell you to make sure that Mercury isn't retrograde when you cast a communication spell and to wait until Venus rises in right ascension of at least ten arc seconds to cast a love spell. To me, this turns spellwork into a mathematical equation; all elements must be present to get the correct answer, and what happens if something isn't quite right? You feel like your spell might fail, and by now you understand what that means—it *will* fail.

If you feel it's time to cast a spell, I suggest that you don't overthink it by examining star charts and books. Yes, making sure that Venus is rising and not setting makes for a powerful love spell. But it doesn't mean that your love spell won't work just because you cast it at noon on Tuesday and didn't wait until 10:00 p.m. when Venus rose. Most important is your intent and the energy you imbue into your working—far more important, in my opinion, than using the "correct" times and astrological correspondences. Don't hinder yourself with doubts that the spell won't work simply because one element wasn't as perfect as it might have been.

If you are concerned about keeping to astrological correspondences, then by all means do so. If you believe that casting a spell only works when you call in god or goddess energy, or if you utilize a circle, then by all means do so. The idea here is to harness *what works*, not to overcomplicate your life with arbitrary rules. My great-grandmother taught me that all that matters is the intent. If the intent is present, the chances of casting a successful spell are much greater than if you are following someone else's rules and don't really understand why. Part of being a witch is understanding what works for you, personally, and why.

I have a close friend who is a numerologist. When she writes her spells, she ensures that the words break down into the number approximating her intent. This works extremely well for her because she believes in the power and meaning of those numbers. On the other hand, I don't, and if I tried to follow her spellcasting technique, I'd probably get disappointing results because I don't really understand or believe in what I'm doing.

As another example, I always harvest plants for use in spellwork first thing in the morning, and the closer to dawn, the better. Why? Because that's when Jeda always gathered hers, that's what she taught me to do, and so far it's worked. Another friend believes in harvesting her plants by moonlight, and her spells work, too. So the question is: does it really matter when you pick your plants? Absolutely! *But only because you give it importance.* If it had never occurred to you before to worry about what time herbs are gathered, why should you worry now? The most important thing to remember is that magical tools have only the power you give them, and their only limits are those you put on them. However, because our minds associate these embellishments with magick, they can be used to make our spellwork more effective. This also means that these embellishments are extras and we can be trained to work without them.

You may ask: if the power isn't in the tools, how does magick work, anyway? As we discussed earlier, all things are surrounded by unique energy fields that vibrate at different frequencies. These fields are susceptible to external and internal forces. Magick manipulates the energy surrounding a particular object to influence a favorable outcome. As witches, we do this in two possible ways—by harnessing and changing the energy surrounding us to invite a reciprocal change, or by attempting to change the energy around others to direct their actions. The latter is dangerous, since it interferes with an individual's free will and invites karmic repercussions. Since the idea of spellwork is to bring about a positive change for ourselves, we need change only the energy surrounding us to sufficiently influence an outcome. Whether or not you use tools and trappings—astrological correspondences, casting a circle, calling on the gods—is up to you.

Let's move on now to practical applications of these concepts. Even though any given spell will have its specific desired outcome, the basics of any magical working should be the same. These basics solidify the connection between the conscious and unconscious parts of our mind so we can, with practice, easily open the magical doors. In short, these basics can be described as intent, items needed (if any), energy, and the best time to cast.

There are two general categories of spells. The first is celebratory, such as those for the Wiccan sabbats and other holidays. Celebratory spells differ greatly by tradition and by the preferences of the individual or group performing them, and can be simple or elaborate, private or public. They are usually designed to honor the god and goddess (or other deities) and to thank them for their help and support in our lives, much like calling home on occasion to talk to Mom and Dad. The god and goddess are invoked or invited into the circle, and although no specific requests are made, a general blessing is usually asked of them. These rites can be simple or elaborate, personal or very public.

EXERCISE 4.3
Writing a celebratory spell

A celebratory spell is written to honor a god or goddess or is written for a particular holiday. It can also be written to celebrate individual milestones, i.e., birthdays or dedications.

For example: Imbolc, also known as Groundhog Day

What is the intent? To celebrate the holiday and say "thank you" for making it through the winter

What will you need: I know that this is a celebration of the coming end of winter, but I also know that winter isn't over yet; this is a time of transition . . . I would use items that represent transition

When: Traditionally Imbolc is celebrated on February 2 of each year, at sunset or sunrise, since those are the times of greatest transition

How would I raise energy? Chant, because that is what we do in the Wiccan tradition I belong to

Your spell might look completely different from mine, but here is one I wrote for Ostara, another Wiccan holiday:

Explanation

Ostara (spring equinox) is celebrated in late March. This is one of two days in the year where night and day are equal in length. Our ancestors came together to celebrate the return of the sun, and to plant their crops for the year as it is the first day of spring.

This holiday falls during Lent, the Christian forty days of fasting leading up to Easter, which is celebrated a mere week after Ostara. In ancient times, this early part of spring was a lean time for ancient pagans. The crops that sustained them through the winter were almost gone, the cupboards were bare, and, since the planting was only just started, there were no fresh foods available. The rites they celebrated for this holiday served to remind them that better things were on the horizon. Spring was coming and with it new hope and a harvest.

The modern belief that eggs are delivered by a rabbit known as the Easter Bunny comes from the legend of the goddess Eostre. So much did a lowly rabbit want to please the goddess that he laid the sacred eggs in her honor, gaily decorated them, and humbly presented them to her. So pleased was she that she wished all humankind to share in her joy. In honor of her wishes, the rabbit went through the entire world and distributed these little decorated gifts of life.

Intent

The joining together of the goddess and god, in keeping with the theme of the day. This holiday concerns the deity's trip to the underworld, and their struggle to return from the land of the dead to Earth. When they accomplish this return, they have a life renewed.

The rite

Call in the quarters.

Practice tonal invocation to raise energy of both the god and goddess together. As the names of the god and goddess merge into one continuous sound, we begin to truly feel their presence in our circle and in our lives. We celebrate their reunion after the long winter months spent in the underworld, the land of the dead. Life is returning to the world as the gods return to us. When the invocation is complete, light the black-and-white candle as a symbol of their tangible presence among us.

Ostara is about starting the crop cycle again. Our ancestors have just planted their crops for the year. They have placed their hopes and wishes for the future in the hands of the gods. They hope that their crops will grow and provide an excellent harvest, that the gods will watch over them and make sure that there will be no famine or blights, and that the land will grant them bounty and abundance. Today, in honor of our ancestors, we too are going to plant seeds of what we desire in the coming seasons.

In keeping with the energy work we did earlier, we are going to charge these candles with our desires and our goals for the coming harvest. As you take the candle in your hand, think about what you want the most—that thing that needs to manifest in your life, the goal you are working so hard to reach. Direct the energy of your hopes into the candle. Take a moment to really focus on what you want, be it love, money, a new job, new direction, insight, spirituality, or just a new connection. Know that by lighting your candle and letting it burn down, you've planted the first seeds for your coming harvest and that the lord and lady will watch over your seeds just as they watched over the seeds planted by our ancestors.

The priestess will take the god/goddess candle and light each of the individual candles, to add divine energy to the personal energy already invested.

Once all the candles have been lit, the priestess will return the candle to the altar.

Thank the lord and lady.

Banish the quarters.

Request spells

Request spells are somewhat different from celebratory spells. A request spell has a very specific goal and is held with the intent of reaching that goal. Here are a few basic rules of thumb for writing a request spell.

1. Every element in the spell—every physical object and every action—should have a meaning. If you aren't sure why you are including something, it doesn't need to be there.

2. Be clear and precise in your stated goal, asking for exactly what you want in as few words as possible. It helps if the words rhyme, but only because the rhythm of the words also contributes to raising energy. If the words don't rhyme, it's okay. It's more important that they're to the point and spoken with feeling.

3. Spells can be cast at any time of the day or night. It's important that you choose a time when you're in the right frame of mind, when you aren't feeling rushed, and when you will not be disturbed.

4. Although complicated astrological correspondences are beyond the scope of this book, at the bare minimum you should be aware of the phases of the moon, as well as moonrise, moonset, and zenith when spellcasting. This isn't a necessity, but

I have found that my spells work much better if I pay attention to these elements. You can find the moon phases, and times of moonrise and moonset in your area, in specialized astrological calendars or online.

a. New moon: The period when the moon in the sky is not visible at all. Best for dispelling negativity, spellbreaking, closing out cycles and starting over.

b. Waxing moon: The period between the new moon and the full moon, when the moon in the sky appears to be increasing in size. Best for attraction magick, situations where you want to draw in new energies or experiences or bring something into manifestation.

c. Full moon: The period when the moon is fully visible—that is, completely round. Best for heavy-duty spells or especially important needs. This is the time when the moon provides the most energy. You can do both banishing and attracting magick during the full moon. It's important here to pay attention to the times of moonrise and moonset when working with full moon energy.

d. Waning moon: The period between the full moon and the new moon, when the moon in the sky appears to be decreasing in size. Best for banishings and generally getting rid of things.

e. Moonrise: The time at which the moon appears above the horizon. Best for attraction magick; works best when coupled with a waxing moon.

f. Moonset: The time at which the moon disappears below the horizon. Best for banishing magick; works best when coupled with a waning moon.

g. Zenith: The highest point in the sky that the moon reaches in its apparent orbit. Like the full moon, it is best for heavy-duty spells, and works best when coupled with the full moon.

5. Try to use fresh ingredients as much as possible. Herbs, even dried ones, have a limited shelf life that can affect their potency. This is particularly true in kitchen magick, where you usually eat or drink the results. Try to replace herbs at least every six months.

6. Energy tip: Sometimes when working through a celebratory rite, it is easy to forget to add the energy. I recommend chanting as a good way of raising and directing energy into the rite. If you are working with a particular deity, a simple and very effective way to raise energy in the rite is simply to chant the name of the deity. Start off softly and slowly, and then build the chant upwards, raising your voice and increasing the speed of the chant as the energy grows. Make sure that, if you are working in a group, you follow the cues of the person directing the chant. If you are the director, it will be up to you to raise the volume and speed of the chant. Do this by raising your own voice and speed, and those around you will follow your lead. Also, as a leader, ensure that you are channeling the energy so that it moves around the circle or so that it settles in the cauldron.

Writing a simple spell

A simple spell is meant to assist the witch in attaining a single, specific goal within a stated time period. Based on what you've learned thus far, write a simple spell for the following example:

Intent: Obtain two hundred dollars, beyond what you need for your regular expenses, to buy a new iPod within the next thirty days

Items needed: Cauldron, paper and pen, lighter or matches

Method of raising energy: Chant

When to cast: When moon is waxing

Write your spell here:

_____

_____

_____

_____

_____

_____

This is how I would perform this spell:

Intent: Same as above
Items needed: Same as above
Method of raising energy: Chant "bring me money"
When to cast: Moonrise during the waxing moon; in
   my location, anytime between 6 a.m. and noon

Steps

Write "$200 for new iPod" on a piece of paper and place it in the cauldron. While chanting, use the technique from exercise 3.7 to visualize energy being drawn into the cauldron and into the paper. Infuse this energy with your intent to draw money; visualize the energy turning green as it becomes saturated with your intent. Release the energy by burning the paper.

This is an example of what may be the simplest spell you will ever cast. Many of my spells are variations on this basic idea. Although I do occasionally like to dance around my cauldron, chanting seems to work best for this type of spell because I don't have to stop what I'm doing, thus disrupting the energy, to burn the paper.

Of course, not every spell will be this simple. Let's try a more complex one:

Writing a more complex spell

This differs from exercise 4.3 in that it has more than one stated goal.

Intent: Either to get promoted at your present job or to find a better job within six months

Items needed: One green candle to represent money, one purple candle to represent positive attention, cauldron or fire-safe plate, paper and pen, lighter or matches, salt

Method of raising energy: Follow the directions in exercise 3.9 to charge the candles

When to cast: When moon is waxing or full

Write your spell here:

_____

_____

_____

_____

_____

_____

_____

This is how I would perform this spell:

Intent: Same as above

Items needed: Same as above

Method of raising energy: Charge green candle to draw money; charge purple candle to attract positive attention

When to cast: At the zenith of the waxing moon. In my location, just after noon

Steps

On the paper, write "I want a better job or a promotion at my present job, with a higher salary, within six months." Set up the candles on a fireproof surface and place the fire-safe plate or cauldron between them. With the salt, draw a circle around the candles to contain their energy (salt is a natural energy barrier). Place the paper on the plate or in the cauldron.

Take a moment to quiet your mind and get centered. When you're ready, light the candles and visualize the energy from them swirling around within the barrier of the salt circle. See the energy rising from each candle, green to draw money, purple to draw favorable attention; meld the two intents together in your mind's eye until they become one. More money, positive recognition, a new job or better position at your present job: this is the goal. Keep this idea at the front of your mind. Visualize yourself getting the better job; what would it look like? How would it feel to have more money and more validation? Make sure the image is clear in your mind.

Next, set the paper on fire, lighting one end with the green candle and the other with the purple candle. Let the paper burn to ashes, and allow the candles to burn down and go out naturally.

Writing a perpetual spell

A perpetual, or ongoing, spell runs over the course of several days or weeks and is not performed all at once. It is best suited for long-term goals, or for something that might take a long time and lots of effort to accomplish.

Try writing a spell for the following example:

Intent: To attract a new lover within the next thirty days

Items needed: One red candle for passion, one pink candle for romantic love, paper and pen, lighter or matches

Method of raising energy: Follow the directions in exercise 3.9 to charge the candles

When to cast: Start when moon is waxing or full

Write your spell here:

_____

_____

_____

_____

_____

This is how I would perform this spell:

Intent: Same as above

Items needed: Same as above

Method of raising energy: Charge red candle to attract passion; charge pink candle to attract romantic love

When to cast: At moonrise during the full moon. About 6 p.m. in my location

Steps

On the paper, write the attributes you want in a lover. Be as specific as possible: "Within the next thirty days, bring me a male lover who is compatible, employed, and emotionally available, who has a good sense of humor." Follow the instructions from exercise 4.4 (you can omit the salt, unless desired) light both candles, and set the paper on fire using the pink candle. While the pink candle burns, focus on directing its energy of attraction into the red candle. When you're ready, extinguish the red candle using a snuffer. Let the pink candle burn down completely to release its energy. Over the coming days, burn the red candle a little at a time, before each time you go out. This reinforces the intent of the spell and puts you in the right frame of mind to attract a lover.

Summary

Most traditional spell books are arranged in alphabetical order, usually with a short preface about the author's qualifications and perhaps a bit of anecdotal information about his, her, or their background. Seldom do you find anything unique—well, perhaps there will be a new way to cast a love spell, or perhaps the book will direct you to drink mint tea and have a conversation with your long-dead grandmother. Of course, my grandmother never cared for mint tea—she would have much rather talked over an extra-sweet cup of Turkish coffee served in petite gold-rimmed cups passed down across three generations.

At the same time that these books provide instruction on moon phases, basic herbology, magickal uses for innocuous household items, and thirty-two ways to get him to fall for you, the books fail the reality test. I mean this in all seriousness and with a great deal of bitter earnestness. I fail to see how simply lighting a candle, drinking tea, and looking into a mirror will conjure my grandmother.

The authors of these books will probably point out that it was my belief—or rather, my lack thereof—in the power of their instructions that assured my failures instead of any lack on their end. Maybe they are right; what I do know is that if you have gotten this far into this book, those types of spell books did not work for you any more than they did for me. As I have said before, that does not mean they are not useful—actually they are very useful in creating a foundation from which to build an actual and successful spell.

Then there are those other books—you know the ones I mean. They loom larger than life on the shelf at the bookstore. They sit with their intimidating covers and thick, uncracked spines daring you to cross the boundary between the mundane and magickal and to embrace a new way of looking at things. These books focus on the spiritual aspects of a religious tradition. Their goal, much like the goal of the Bible or the Qur'an, is to assist their followers in creating a dogma, a set of spiritual ideals, beliefs, and practices that guide moral and spiritual development. These books inform the reader about the ramifications of spellcasting, about the drawbacks of interfering with free will, and yet at the same time they also promise to provide enlightenment, self-worth, and inner peace. They do not promise that Bob in accounting will notice you, or that Phil, the new manager in human resources, will promote you. Instead they focus on teaching individual readers how to be happy with what they have—to live with the hand they have been dealt, so to speak. To me, these books bind people with one hand while promising to release them from their chains with the other.

My grandmother, much to the chagrin of my father, would consult an astrologer monthly. My father always said that if she had to choose between food and going to the astrologer, she would go to the astrologer, no contest. My grandmother would say that the food would take care of it-self—after all, Allah would provide. The wisdom and insight provided by the astrologer, of course, would be essential to determine the best way that the food would be provided now that the money was gone. (I don't believe that it ever came down to a choice between food or astrology, though.)

Still, I cannot discount the power and energy found in true faith. When I first moved to the United States, I lived in a rural Michigan town; there were three churches on each corner but not a single mosque in three counties. My friends were Christian, my mother's family Christian, the public school was filled with Christian overtones—after-school Bible study, youth group, prayer before choir con-certs and football games. I was inundated with all things Christian, and it was not long before I found myself going to church on Sunday. The thing I remember most clearly about church was how some churches felt different from others. In some churches I walked in and felt absolutely nothing. In other churches, before I even set foot in them, I felt the hum of energy and the feeling of peace, and faith emanated into the parking lot. These places felt like the old mosques in Amman, where generation upon genera-tion of the faithful walked in and bowed down in worship of an entity or idea greater than themselves.

One of the first things that people always ask me when they hear about my background and family history is "And you became a witch *how?*" It is almost inconceivable to them that a person from an Islamic background would choose Wicca as her religion, and they are even more shocked when I tell them that the ideas of Wicca and witchcraft are not incompatible with those of the big three religions.

As a child I loved stories, being told them and creating my own. I was an impatient child, wanting to know everything, wanting to understand the *why* behind things. By the time I was four, I'd been banned from the local mosque in Amman for arguing with the sheik. By fifteen I was reading the works of Diane Stein, Starhawk, and Scott Cunningham, and I was reinventing my world in a way that finally made sense. Finally, by twenty, I realized that much of what I did as child, what I learned from the women of my family, was preparing me for rediscovering the Goddess and the power of the feminine within Islamic society. At twenty-two, I had the opportunity to go to Egypt, to walk in the temples of Isis and Hathor, to visit the great Pyramids and the old cities of the pharaohs. As I walked there, in Luxor, Cairo, Aswan, and Alexandria, I felt the echoes of the ancient power beneath my feet. The images of the goddesses flowed across the landscape of my inner eye. Just being there in Egypt was like being in a different world. It was while I was there that I first became introduced to traditional Islamic mysticism and the practices of Sufism.

The cornerstone of Sufi belief is "God is love." That seems like a simple concept, but it really isn't. The idea is a rejection of the fear taught in traditional Islam; it is a rejection of the power over mentality. It is the idea that a person should seek union with God/Allah not because of the fear of punishment or the promise of rewards, but rather because of love. The union of man and God in this tradition is compared to a marriage. In order for a marriage to work, you have to have balance, understanding, and love; neither party should be over the other. Instead, it should function as a partnership. To take this a step further, I would even say that each party has to be equal in the relationship for it work. This is a revolutionary idea, because it changes the relationship between man and deity from overlord and servant to an equal partnership. It is all about an exchange of power.

The main issue between the practice of witchcraft and following one of the traditional big three religions is who is in the driver's seat. As a witch, I am in control; it is my words, my will, and my thoughts that carry the power. As a Christian/Muslim/Jew, it is the will of God that rules, and my will sublimates itself to the will of this God—this means that if my life sucks, I beg someone else to listen and fix it, instead of taking action and fixing it myself. The thing I like most about Wicca is that I still get to be in the driver's seat, I shape my own destiny, and the gods/goddesses are there to help me and not to punish me for wanting more from life.

So what does this have to do with energy?

What it means is that each person has the ability to create his or her own universe, albeit on a lesser scale than Allah is capable of, since his power is not diluted or restricted within flesh. It also means that when a person dies his or her rooh is set free and returns to Allah until the Day of Judgment.

To some, being given a portion of Allah's power in the form of a soul is considered a divine mandate by God to use this power, even though it is contrary to the idea that humans should submit to the will and power of Allah. Or is it? After all, Allah would not have given you power if he didn't want you to use it. Perhaps it is a test? Still, a person must be cognizant of the idea that though Allah uses the power for creation, he can also use it for destruction. So people must be very careful in using their power. So careful, in fact, that many people have given up the right to use this power because they feel that their judgment can never be as sound as that of an all-knowing divinity. They give up this personal power and trust that Allah knows best. Essentially, they become sheep, if only figuratively. They submit their own judgment to that of Allah by choosing to follow Allah's rules. (Think of the Ten Commandments or the rule of three, or the Wiccan Rede.)

Allah/God/etc. gave humans power and the ability to use this power if they so choose. It also means that people have the right to choose not to use this power, even though it might make life harder for them. Think Job. If you choose to use the power granted to you by the divine, then it is important to understand it, to realize its potential, and to weigh the consequences of your choices. By choosing to use the power, you give up the safety net, the protection of ignorance, and you make an informed decision. The power granted to humanity is a right of creation; it accepts that the God of Abraham is real and that the cosmology associated with it is also real. It also means that, as a witch, you are working without a net, and this can make you vulnerable to external energies, which can influence, affect, or even disrupt spellwork.

The Christian solution: don't practice magick. The traditional Muslim solution: leave the magick to those who know what they're doing. The Wiccan solution: work in a circle. There is a bit of a dispute as to exactly how a magickal circle should function, and if the witch should be within or without the circle at the time of spellcasting. This difference can be traced back to the earliest foundations of Wicca, and I have no solution except to say do what feels right to you. In my own workings I tend to stay within the confines of the circle, unless I am doing work for someone else, at which point I am outside the circle, and the energy is directed by me within the circle (this sounds more complex than it actually is).

The first step in either case is the same: establish the circle by determining the boundaries and then reinforcing the boundaries with energy. Any introductory book to Wicca will instruct you in the basics of circle casting. If you choose to follow those instructions, then do so and add the following. If you choose not to follow those instructions, then either create your own, or simply follow the four simple steps outlined here:

1. Ground by extending and entwining your energy with that of the earth.

2. Next, direct energy upward in four tendrils from the earth until they push out like small growing trees at each corner point of the circle (one at north, east, south, and west, respectively). You can think of them as posts or spikes instead of trees if that helps.

3. Finally, direct the energy from each tree. Picture branches growing out and flowing first around the circle and then upward until they intertwine and form a lattice of energy all around the circle boundaries and above. From below, direct the

energy from the roots to form another intertwined network of roots beneath the earth.

4. From the branches, direct the energy again until all the branches are seamlessly woven together without any gaps or breaks—to the external eye it will appear as a glowing ball of light. If you are within the circle, you should feel the hum of the energy surrounding you.

Once you have completed your spell or ritual, take down the circle by first pulling back all the roots and branches into the trunk of your energy tree, and then slowly release the four tendrils back into the earth. Finally, untangle your energy from that of the earth as directed in prior exercises.

five

Other Useful Techniques

Kitchen Magick

There is another method of spellcasting that I want to briefly touch on: kitchen magick. My great-grandmother was essentially a kitchen witch. Yes, she made charms, read palms and tea leaves, and even analyzed horoscopes. But where she really shone was in the kitchen. She knew what every herb in her pantry was for.

The basic idea behind kitchen magick is to imbue the intent of your working into the food or drink you and others will consume. This means paying attention to what will taste good, of course, but also to the effects of each ingredient, both on its own and when combined. Kitchen witchery harnesses the fact that everyone has to eat, and combines it with the idea that anything can be a spell if the witch is in the right frame of mind and the ingredients are directed toward a specific intent. In essence, all aspects of life, even the most mundane acts, have the potential to be magical if the witch intends it.

When making dinner each night, I focus on a particular goal or desire. I select herbs based not only on how they will taste but also based on what I believe these herbs can accomplish. You can apply this technique to a main dish, to an entire meal, or to teas, tinctures, and potions that can be consumed, filling both a mundane and magical need. Many books are available that give detailed lists of the properties of herbs as related to both cooking and spellwork.

Just as in this book's exercises, energy is raised and directed in the act of cooking—only it is directed into something that will be consumed. Furthermore, the act of consumption itself can be considered magical, because it transforms a tangible substance into pure energy used to fuel the body—the ultimate magical transformation.

If you have noticed, none of the spells here call in divine or god/goddess energy. That is because I believe that spellwork can be accomplished without divine help. There is a fundamental difference between witchcraft as a skill, which is open to anyone, regardless of religious ideology, and Paganism or Wicca, which have preset dogmas and adhere to a particular spiritual belief structure. Anyone can practice witchcraft; it is a skill set that, once cultivated, will work independently of spirituality. At the same time, though, Paganism—and Wicca in particular—embraces spellwork as an essential aspect of its spiritual traditions.

Generally speaking, Pagans and Wiccans will use many of the spellwork techniques discussed here in their spiritual worship. They find no distinction between magick and spirituality; it is all part of the same parcel to them, until one becomes indistinct from the other.

As a Wiccan, I adhere to some particular aspects of spellcasting that are fundamentally tied to my spiritual beliefs. This may be the case for you, or it may not be. The simple truth of the matter is that it is up to you, as a matter of choice or belief, to elect to work with or work without divine help. If you do choose to work with a particular deity, or a god/goddess pair, make sure that you understand the mythology and mystery tradition associated with the being you choose to work with. Above all else, it is important to ensure that you know what you are calling in! Adding an unknown energy into the spell is asking for trouble. You can't simply call on a generic or random deity without understanding the archetype that deity is associated with. Walking into such a spell is asking for something bad to happen. I know this may sound overly cautionary, but it is extremely important to make sure that you do your research into any entity you plan on calling in, be it divine, elemental, Fae, etc. By doing research, I mean more than reading a short blurb about a goddess or god in a book and then thinking that you understand the complete aspect of what you are calling in.

Do not call on a goddess or god just because you think you need to for the spell to work. In fact, if that is the only reason you are associating with a particular divine entity, you may want to reconsider working with it, and instead choose to work with someone you have a relationship with. Think of it this way: you wouldn't ask a random stranger on the street to come help with your spellcasting, so why do the same with other entities? Working with the divine requires trust and reciprocity; it is not something that should be entered into in a half-assed manner. Do the research, build the relationship, and above all make sure you understand the archetypes you call in, or suffer the consequences. Doing a half-assed job produces half-assed results.

There are hundreds if not thousands of different methods of spellcasting out there. Please make sure you do the research and pick the methods that work best for you. In the end, magick is selfish, and by extension, so are witches. We care about results and about getting what we want. If the methodology you are employing doesn't produce results, then find something that does. The only limits that exist are the ones you place on yourself.

Energy Shields

In chapter 2, we discussed the natural barrier that each person possesses at the edge of his or her energy field. In exercise 2.6, you learned how to combine your energy with a partner and, to do so, you had to consciously lower your barrier. In this section, we will learn a related skill: how to build active and passive energy shields. Passive shields work hand in hand with your natural energy barrier and are kept in place at all times to deflect *general* unwanted energy. Active shields are put in place to keep out *specific* negative energy associated with a person, a group, a place, or a thing. You would use an active shield if you perceived a threat or felt uncomfortable in a particular situation.

Shielding oneself is important for many reasons, not the least of which is protection. The shielding exercises may have many different applications outside of physical protection. As you become more proficient at the exercises, consider focusing on the type of protection you are seeking. Work with the color exercise (3.1) and modify it based on what you need protection from—for example, if you are confronted with a situation that makes you feel depressed, focus your shield to keep out the energy of depression. For me, the color of depression is a dull, almost black gray, the kind that colors the sky before a snowstorm. So I would focus my shield on keeping out energy that feels or carries a similar color or texture, while reinforcing the shield with the emotion I consider to be the opposite of depression—happiness. So your shield would take on the color of happiness as you focus on drawing that particular type of energy in through the shield while blocking the other type of energy you are seeking to avoid. This is a more advanced technique. I recommend working with two other people to perfect it.

Step one: Create the shield as instructed in the prior exercise. This time, focus on keeping out a particular emotion or feeling.

Step two: Have your first partner project the type of energy you are attempting to block with your shield. For this, the partner should meditate on the color and feeling of the energy desired as directed in exercise 3.1. Once this partner has the feeling of the energy mastered, he or she should direct it outward toward the shield created. You should focus on keeping out the energy being directed at you. Once you are sure that you are blocking the energy, proceed to step three.

Step three: Have the second partner direct the opposite emotion at you (you should decide what this emotion will be). The second partner should meditate on the feeling and the color of the energy prior to projecting it outward, just as the first partner did. Focus on allowing this energy through the shield while keeping out the negative energy you choose to block.

You may want to switch off and repeat the exercise more than once until you are sure that you have it down.

Another important aspect of shielding is deflection—that is, showing others only what you want them to see. Think of it as magical camouflage. You see, working with energy creates a resonance that other practitioners can sense. I don't know about you, but I don't want every Tom, Dick, and Harry to recognize what I'm capable of. My shields are so successful that a person would not know I was a witch unless I made an announcement (which is unlikely), and even then they might be skeptical. Remember that a cornerstone of magical theory is silence. It's called the craft of the wise, after all, not the craft of the loudmouth! In my experience, those who loudly proclaim their power usually don't have enough of it to fill a thimble. It's the quiet ones you need to be wary of.

The most common type of passive shielding may be the reflective shield, which is like a mirror showing an aggressor a reflection of his energy and directing it back at him. However, some believe that this type of shield encourages confrontation. When an aggressive energy or personality encounters another aggressive energy, even if it is only a reflection, it reacts by wanting to assert dominance, just like a dog would to prove it is the alpha. For that reason, I don't recommend using a reflective shield; instead, I use a diffusive shield. Like a black hole, a diffusive shield sucks in the negative energy it encounters rather than reflecting it back. People who use this type of shielding emit little personal energy and are not easy to "read." If you were to attempt to touch their energy field, you would hit what feels like a black, sucking void.

I reinforce my passive shield each morning; others may do it once a week or once a month; still others will take a "set it and forget it" approach. My recommendation is to reinforce your defenses periodically, based on how much negativity you encounter. You will learn what works best for you.

EXERCISE 5.1

Creating a passive shield

For this exercise you will need:
   About five minutes daily

Sit comfortably in a place where you won't be disturbed. Take a moment to locate the edge of your energy field, as you did in exercise 2.6. By this point, you should be able to easily locate it. Now visualize a transparent film that settles directly over your natural barrier and conforms to its size and shape. Once the film is in place, see it becoming like a sponge that will absorb any negativity it encounters. As it sucks up negativity, it alters that energy and neutralizes it, like an antibacterial killing germs.

Now you have a choice as to what to do with the absorbed energy. You can visualize the sponge shield wringing itself out and directing the energy into the earth. If you use this approach, be sure to check the shield occasionally to make sure that it is still working as intended. Or, you can do what I do and allow the neutralized energy to slowly seep through the sponge shield until it melds with my own energy field. You might feel a little concerned about doing this, but remember that energy itself is not good or bad, it is neutral. When you remove the ill intent or negativity from energy directed toward you, it becomes as "clean" as energy you've raised yourself, and it requires no effort on your part. I think there's no better revenge on a person who wishes you harm than taking the energy he or she has invested in hating you and using it to meet your own goals.

As you conclude setting your passive shield, take a moment to scan your energy field for any lingering negativity or other unwanted energy, and return it to the earth as you did in exercise 2.7.

Sometimes you run into such negativity that your passive shields are no longer sufficient. You will encounter people that you just can't neutralize enough; they are bad news and you can often tell just by looking at them. There will also be times when you find yourself in situations where you feel threatened or unsafe. You know the scene:

You're walking alone down a dark street. It's late and the area is not the best. You hear footsteps behind you, and you tell yourself it's nothing. You pick up the pace, clutch your purse closer. It's important not to discount your gut feelings in these circumstances; these are instinctual warnings telling you to be aware. In addition to a healthy dose of common sense—get yourself out of the situation as quickly as possible—some extra shielding may be needed.

EXERCISE 5.2

Creating an active shield

For this exercise you will need:

Five minutes

Active shields are custom made for a specific set of circumstances. The premise behind them is very simple: you want to put a "wall" of energy between yourself and the threat. The type of wall you create will depend on the situation, and will usually need to be created almost instantaneously, without visible effort.

Let's walk through an example. If you move within a Wiccan or Pagan community, you will occasionally come into contact with someone you don't even want to be around, let alone share energy with. But it's a full moon, your friend is leading an open, public celebration circle, and you promised you would participate. So what do you do?

In this case, you might want to picture a brick wall going up between you and him or her. You will need to focus on keeping out only the energy of that particular person, while at the same time staying open to the energy from the rest of the group. Selectively letting in some energy while keeping out other energy takes practice and concentration. In another example, let's go back to that deserted street where you heard footsteps in the dark. Rather than visualizing a solid barrier like a brick wall, I suggest projecting a shroud or veil of energy around you, which you use to blend in and become unnoticeable. This technique works very well if you do nothing to attract attention to yourself. Walk away from the threat at a steady pace, visualizing a night-colored sheet covering you from head to toe. Focus on the word "invisible." Repeat it like a chant in your mind, in rhythm with your footsteps, actively concentrating on being unseen until you reach your car or other place of safety.

The type of shield you choose to project in this situation may depend on your personality. For example, a man might choose to appear threatening or physically larger, so the mugger is intimidated into leaving him alone. However, keep in mind that if you project an aura of menace, you risk a confrontation, as we discussed earlier.

Learning to set up an active shield "on the run" takes some time and effort. Obviously you won't want to put yourself in harm's way to practice, but try creating a wall between yourself and the grouchy cashier at the grocery store, or making yourself invisible to the local traffic patrol. You can also use an active shield to change people's perceptions of you, almost like a mask. This technique is often called a glamour. Rather than projecting invisibility, as above, you project a particular characteristic to influence others' perceptions of you. You're actively altering what a person will notice about you, allowing people to see you only in the way you intend.

In the movie *The Craft*, Sarah used a glamour to change her hair color and Nancy used one to make everyone think she was Sarah. I must admit, I have yet to meet someone who is actually able to do this. On the other hand, it's fairly easy to encourage a boyfriend, for example, to see you as being wildly attractive. This technique can be really useful on job interviews and first dates, although it doesn't work as successfully on people who know you well.

EXERCISE 5.3

Creating a glamour

For this exercise you will need:

About five minutes

A mirror

An outfit that corresponds with your goal

A related object such as a piece of jewelry

This exercise has two parts: creating a connection between the image you want to project and the object you choose for a charm, then creating the illusion itself.

The first thing you need to ask is: what exactly do you want to project? Just as the wording you choose for your spells needs to be clear and specific, so does the goal for your glamour. If you are trying to project competence, for a job interview as an example, you really need to see competence in your mind's eye. To me, a competent person is well dressed; he or she wears professional clothes like a suit. Visualize someone who looks like you wearing a charcoal gray suit with a crisp white blouse (or shirt). Her (or his) hair is neatly styled, either cut short or pulled back into a bun. She walks with purpose, not in a hurry but not wasting time. Her face is pleasant but impassive, not smiling or frowning. When she speaks, each word is carefully chosen, giving just the right amount of information. She carries a small notepad in which to write things down.

The second thing you need to ask is: what object represents this image and its corresponding emotion? I might choose a pearl necklace to represent competence, because it is classic and, when I wear it, I feel elegant. It's easier for me to see that competent woman in the gray suit wearing pearls than it is to see her wearing a gaudy piece of costume jewelry.

The final thing you need to ask is: what color do you associate with this image and its emotion? I might choose gray, because that charcoal suit is a classic that will never go out of style.

As we discussed in exercise 3.1, you have your own innate set of colors that correspond to emotions. You also have your own ideas how competence might be symbolized or represented, so there's no right or wrong way to do this exercise. However, it's important to have that image fixed in your mind, because you want to draw on the energy of the emotion. The clearer the image is to you, the easier it is for you to connect with its energy and project it outward.

At this point, put on the outfit you chose that represents competence to you. Put on make-up and style your hair, too. You will want to dress as closely as possible to your idealized image (it's hard to project competence in cut-offs and a tank top). Once you are dressed, stand in front of the mirror and look directly into your own eyes.

Hold the image of yourself in the mirror in your mind's eye. When you're sure the image is fixed there, close your eyes. Can you visualize how you looked in the mirror? If you can't, try again until you can clearly see your reflection standing in front of you in your mind's eye.

Now bring back your image of the personification of competence, that capable person in the classic charcoal gray suit. Place the image of you in the mirror next to her. Slowly start bringing them together, superimposing one on top of the other, like an out-of-focus image becoming clearer. Merge your image from the mirror with the image you created until they are totally blended. Now *you* are the personification of competence.

Open your eyes and focus on the image in the mirror. See the blended image you created there and focus on it until it's clear. See it superimposed over your reflection in the mirror. Doing this will get easier and quicker with practice; if you don't see it at first, keep trying. Don't be surprised if it looks like an out-of-focus version of you or a multilayered you.

The glamour will last as long as you wear the outfit. If you happen to walk past a mirror, you should bring up the image you created for reinforcement.

You can do this spell without the piece of jewelry to serve as a charm, but when you are new to casting this type of illusion, you sometimes needs a tangible reminder of the image you are projecting. I have a necklace that I wear every time I go on a job interview; when I wear it, I feel more confident, capable, and skilled. I also have a bracelet that I like to wear when going out; it makes me feel sexy and beautiful. I have friends who keep stones or other charms in their pockets for the same reason. All they have to do is touch them to regain their focus. Sometimes I think of them like Dumbo's feather—a touchstone that allows you to access your own potential. After all, Dumbo flew without his feather in the end. You can also go one step further and charge your reminder object with energy to make it an active charm, as you did in exercise 3.10.

six

Ten Practical Tips

Tip One

There is an adage in Wicca that encourages a person "to know, to will, to dare, and to keep silent." In my opinion, this is one of the most important statements in modern witchcraft.

To know is to learn everything you can about your craft. Master it, or it will master you.

To will is to take action and use the skills you have learned.

To dare is to follow through on what you willed. This means continually putting energy into your desired outcome: visualizing favorable results, keeping a positive attitude, and taking the real-world actions that will help the spell along. A spell without follow-through is a spell half-done, and one that will not be successful.

To keep silent is the hardest to explain. Many consider this an invitation to become a closet dweller, but I don't think so. This is simply a reminder that not everyone needs to know your business. As we discussed, the energy of a spell can easily be overwhelmed by a countering energy. Thus it's extremely important not to discuss your magical workings with those who may have a negative attitude about the magick itself, or about the possibility of its success.

Some witches embrace magick for the purpose of shocking or frightening mundane people, and their use of power is like a club—blunt, brutal, and swift. I think of them as the cavemen of witchcraft. Their power lacks depth and they disclose their actions to everyone. I prefer to use power (energy) more subtly. Think of magick as being like an assassin's dagger; it's carefully wielded, precisely targeted, and you never it see it coming until it slides between your ribs. Good assassins don't stand out; they blend in, and you don't know who they are or what they are up to. Be cautious whom you share your secrets with.

Tip Two

Always make a spell your own. Don't just follow the instructions someone else gives you without understanding them and agreeing with them. You should feel comfortable and connected when doing any type of working. If anything makes you feel uncomfortable or disconnected, stop or make a change. For example, most magick books say to use black candles to dispel negativity. Those same books also say to use black candles to represent the god aspect of Wicca's divine duality. I don't like using a candle whose color represents negativity to honor my god, so instead I use a red candle.

Effective spellwork is a process of trial and error. The best thing about this path is that there is no preset formula, but also the worst thing is that there is no preset formula. A + B = C is not going to work for each individual, so don't feel bad if you don't connect with a technique, a theory, or an element used in a spell.

Tip Three

Complicated isn't always more powerful. Don't be afraid to let some of your items do double duty if needed.

The idea is to have a connection between the mundane and etheric, this can be anything. You can cast a great spell with nothing more than intent. Everything else is just window dressing.

Tip Four

Be clear and precise in the stated goal of a spell. Ask for what you want or need, and remember that magick takes the path of least resistance. Also, don't be afraid to speak from the heart. I can't rhyme to save my life. It is better to have a specific well-worded, unrhymed spell, than to have a rhymed piece of junk.

Tip Five

Ask for what you want or need. Magick is not going to read your mind and just give it to you. Even if it could why would it bother? Magick/energy takes the path of least resistance. Sometimes that can be right over you, don't let that happen.

Tip Six

Don't overthink things. It is good to look at what can go wrong or what the possible consequences of a spell can be. But don't let fear of what can happen stop you from taking action. Doing nothing can be worse. You need to trust your judgment.

Remember that the minute doubt creeps in all your hard work goes down the toilet.

Tip Seven

Don't listen to naysayers and doubters. There are always people who either underestimate you or put you down just because they can. Don't listen. You are powerful! If they can't get behind that idea, then put them behind you.

Tip Eight

If at first you don't succeed try again, and again. Don't let an initial setback stop you. Sometimes the twenty-sixth time is the charm.

Tip Nine

Ask for help if you need it. No one can do everything alone.

Tip Ten

RELAX! Trust yourself.

Good Luck!

seven

Guided Meditations

THE PURPOSE OF THE FOLLOWING meditations is to assist you in opening up your inner eye. This should help if you are having trouble with focus or with the other visualization techniques in the rest of the book. The goal of these two meditations is to walk you through the visualization process from beginning to end. This process should familiarize you with the necessary steps you will need to master before moving on to some of the more complex exercises. It will also assist you in focusing your inner eye.

I recommend recording the visualizations and replaying them or doing them as part of a group exercise; reading the visualizations will not be enough to experience the full effect.

Prior to each meditation, you should allow yourself to relax. Either sit or lie back somewhere comfortable where you will not be disturbed.

Guided Meditations

1. The forest (discovering your gifts)

Begin by sitting comfortably upright, back straight, with your hands resting palm down on your knees.

Breathe deeply, inhale through your nose, slowly . . . one, two, three . . . exhale through your mouth, and as you exhale, feel the tension leaving your body. Inhale clean, deep breaths, exhale, and relax. Inhale . . . three, two, one . . . exhale. (Repeat.) Relax the tension in your body. Feel your muscles relax, starting with your shoulders and moving down to the soles of your feet. Breathe and relax.

Once you're relaxed, reach inward and open your third eye. You find yourself in a small grassy clearing surrounded by trees. You can hear birds singing and the wind whispering through the leaves. You feel the sun's warmth on your face. Take a moment to enjoy the scene. When you're ready, begin walking through the clearing toward the woods. With each step you feel more and more removed from the mundane, and as you continue to walk toward the woods you feel an increasingly deeper connection to the spiritual world.

As you near the woods, you begin to see a narrow path emerge. This path will guide you through the woods. It is darker in the woods and very green. Large trees form a canopy of green above you, the sun shines down through the leaves, and the world feels very ethereal. You see small animals and birds playing along the path. You continue walking past the animals, under the birds, walking down the path. The forest becomes denser around you, and the path becomes more and more narrow, almost as if the trees are trying to hide something from view. But you continue your journey, walking at a steady pace.

Eventually you reach what seems to be the end of the path, and you see a great living oak tree. This tree sits directly in your path, and you cannot go around. Hanging from this tree you find a bag—this is just within your reach. You take the bag and open it. As you peer into the open bag, you notice a bright white light shinning out. In this light there is a message for you. See this message, understand it, and memorize it. When you are sure you understand the message, close the bag and return it to the tree.

As you turn to leave, you thank the tree and the gods for the message. You walk through the forest again on the narrow path back past the animals and the birds. As you come through the woods and into the clearing, you return to the awareness of the mundane world you left behind. You feel the rise and fall of your chest, the inhalation through your nose and exhalation through your mouth. But you are still relaxed, and you feel at peace. When you are ready to leave the clearing, open your eyes. You have returned.

2. The dream

Begin by following the first steps of meditation one in order to achieve a state of relaxation.

Close your eyes and open your inner vision. You find yourself in a new place. It is the brightest blue day, the sun hangs low in the east, and there is a gentle warm breeze on your face. You are wearing no shoes, and for once you don't worry. You walk along a beach enclosed by singing rocks on three sides, and you feel at peace. Make your way slowly, meandering up a path to the top of a hill, and look down. You see a green city spread out in serene glory, with the pillars of a mud-brick temple standing out in the background. In this place you see no garbage, no death, no famine, and no war. It is perfect and it is beautiful and peaceful, and you are alone. You turn to begin making your way down back to the beach when you see someone waiting for you. At first you don't want to go meet him, but something compels your feet forward.

You stand before a man and he smiles. You just look at him. "I have been waiting for you," he says, and the two of you begin to stroll.

For a while he doesn't say anything, and then you are both back looking out at the city. "I have wanted to see you, ever since I've known you were coming. I have been to this place," he says waving at the city below you; it sparkles in the sun, glowing and almost golden.

It is a place you have been to before also: Aswan. Not the Aswan as it is today, with its derelict houses, crumbling temples, armed escorts surrounding what few tourists there are. No, this place is more than beautiful. It is surreal—the temples of gods so long neglected shine glimmering in the sun, whole and unaffected by the vagaries of time. There are no derelict houses, no white washed hotels with rooftop pools. The streets are paved with stone instead of pitted asphalt. The sidewalks are lined with stately lions instead of demanding merchants.

A procession of men walks along the street, moving unhurriedly to the golden-hued temple in the distance. The Nile glitters a bright blue in the sun, and fertile fields of green serve to showcase it edged with the deepest green that gives way suddenly to the gold of sand and desert. It snakes to the left of the street, edging toward the temple and then sharply turning away. The two of you stand above it all, watching.

What is this place? Who is this man? Most importantly, why are you here? It is as if he reads your mind, because now he speaks: "I have wanted to share this place with you, but you have forgotten me. All of these things I have made for you, but time erased the memory and this place with it." You feel sad, anguished, that you could have ever forgotten him, the sun, the god Ra.

The time for transformation has come, the time for remembrance; a journey unfolds within the mind of the seeker. Welcome now unto this path.

You awake, and remember.

Suggested Reading and Bibliography

Magick/Spellwork

Ashcroft-Nowicki, Dolores. *Magical Use of Thoughtforms.* St. Paul, MN: Llewellyn, 2001.

Augustine. *The City of God.* Translated by Henry Bettenson. New York: Penguin Classics, 1984.

Buckland, Raymond. *The Complete Book of Witchcraft.* St. Paul, MN: Llewellyn, 2002.

Cooper, Patrinella. *Gypsy Magic.* Newburyport, MA: Weiser, 2002.

Cunningham, Scott. *Earth, Air, Fire, and Water: More Techniques of Natural Magic.* St. Paul, MN: Llewellyn, reprinted 2002.

———. *Earth Power: Techniques of Natural Magic.* St. Paul, MN: Llewellyn, reprinted 2002.

Grimassi, Raven. *Italian Witchcraft.* St. Paul, MN: Llewellyn, 2000.

———. *The Witches' Craft: The Roots of Witchcraft & Magical Transformation.* St. Paul, MN: Llewellyn, 2002.

Kaufman, Walter. *Hegel: A Reinterpretation.* New York: Doubleday, 1966.

Llera, Cora. *Signature Energy Work.* Bangor, ME: Booklocker, 2005.

More, Thomas. *Utopia.* New ed. New Haven, CT: Yale University Press, 2001.

Morrison, Dorothy. *The Craft: A Witch's Book of Shadows.* St. Paul, MN: Llewellyn, 2001.

———. *Everyday Magic: Spells & Ritual for Modern Living.* St. Paul, MN: Llewellyn, 2002.

Stein, Diane. *Casting the Circle: A Woman's Book of Ritual,* Berkeley, CA: Crossing Press, 1990.

Worth, Valerie. *Crone's Book of Charms & Spells.* 2nd ed. St. Paul, MN: Llewellyn, 2002.

Paganism

Adler, Margot. *Drawing Down the Moon: Witches, Druids, Goddess-Worshippers, and Other Pagans in America.* New York: Penguin, 1986.

Harvey, Graham. *Contemporary Paganism: Listening People, Speaking Earth.* New York: New York University Press, 1997.

York, Michael. *Pagan Theology: Paganism as a World Religion.* New York: New York University Press, 2003.

Religion

Gnostic Bible, The. Boston, MA: Shambhala, 2003.

Qur'an, The. English trans. of official Egyptian trans., 1923.

Wicca

Cunningham, Scott. *Living Wicca: A Further Guide for the Solitary Practitioner*. St. Paul, MN: Llewellyn, reprinted 2002.

————. *Wicca: A Guide for the Solitary Practitioner*. St. Paul, MN: Llewellyn, 1993.

Starhawk. *The Spiral Dance: A Rebirth of the Ancient Religion of the Goddess*. 20th anniversary ed. New York: Harper, 1999.